FOR WHOM THE SMELL TOLLS

A NORA BLACK MIDLIFE PSYCHIC MYSTERY
BOOK TWO

RENEE GEORGE

BARKSIDE OF THE MOON PRESS

For Whom The Smell Tolls

A Nora Black, Midlife Psychic Book 2

Print Edition May 2020

ISBN: 978-1-947177-35-2

Publisher: Barkside of the Moon Press

"Sense and Scent Ability by Renee George is a delightfully funny, smart, full of excitement, up-all-night fantastic read! I couldn't put it down. The latest installment in the Paranormal Women's Fiction movement, knocks it out of the park. Do yourself a favor and grab a copy today!"

— —ROBYN PETERMAN NYT
BESTSELLING AUTHOR

"I'm loving the Paranormal Women's Fiction genre! Renee George's humor shines when a woman of a certain age sniffs out the bad guy and saves her bestie. Funny, strong female friendships rule!"

— -- MICHELLE M. PILLOW, NYT & USAT
BESTSELLING AUTHOR

"I smell a winner with Renee George's new book, Sense & Scent Ability! The heroine proves that being over fifty doesn't have to stink, even if her psychic visions do."

"Sense & Scent Ability is everything! Nora Black is sassy, smart, and her smell-o-vision is scent-sational. I can't wait for the next Nora book!

For My BFFs.
You inspire me every day.

ACKNOWLEDGMENTS

A huge thank you to Robyn, Michele, Robbin, and Kelli. It took a village to write this book, and thanks to you, it's awesome. Thank you for being my people!

To the PWF #13 - Thanks for bringing attention to heroines of a certain age. You ladies are magnificent.

My husband Steve and my son Taylor for taking up the slack around the house, and most of all, leaving me alone to write! I literally couldn't do this without you.

And finally, to the readers. You are making this midlife writer happier than you can even imagine! Thank you for loving Nora and going on this journey with her and her BFF brigade.

My name is Nora Black. I'm over fifty and enjoying my life to the fullest. That is, when I'm not worried about graying hair, back pain, allergies, and a psychic gift that sometimes stinks.

After solving a murder with the help of my new scent-induced psychic ability, I'm thrilled to report that everything is finally getting back to normal. Better than normal, actually. My BFFs work with me at my Scents & Scentsability shop, I'm dating a young, hot detective, and the upcoming Memorial Day weekend promises to bring in lots of tourists to Garden Cove.

There's not a thing in this world that could spoil my great mood...

Nothing except a suspicious death. When police officer Reese McKay asks me to use my aroma-mojo to look into the "accidental drowning" of her black-sheep cousin, I can't turn her away. Especially now that she's become a friend.

With help from my besties Gilly and Pippa, along with an unofficial assist from Detective Hot Stuff, I'm determined to crack the case of the drowned girl and sniff out the killer before he or she can strike again.

CHAPTER 1

"*I*'ve made a decision, Nora. You're not going to like it, but I really need you to be okay with it." Gilly Martin, my best friend in the world, hit me with her most earnest gaze. "I hope I'll have your support."

It was five o'clock in the afternoon, and we were finishing the closing cleanup of Scents & Scentsability, my spa boutique in Garden Cove. Since I'd added the massage component, Gilly's part of the business, the sales of our lotions, massage oils, and soaps had doubled.

I shook my head. "Please don't tell me you're pregnant," I said teasingly as I wiped the inside of the front door, but the darkening in Gilly's brown eyes made me gasp. "You're pregnant? How? Why?" I asked, appalled at the idea. "For the love of Pete, you're fifty-one years old, Gillian Judith Martin. You have two teenagers getting ready to start their senior year. Why would you want to start over?"

Gilly's frown deepened for a second, then her lip began to tremble. Was she going to cry?

"I'm sorry!" I said quickly. "Of course, I support you. I'm here for you no matter what."

A choking sound bubbled from her lips as she turned away from me.

"Please don't cry." I was a terrible BFF. Gilly needed my understanding, my patience, my love—not my judgement. "I'll even take those awful Bradley child-birth breathing classes with you if you want."

Now she was in a full-on sob...or at least, I thought.

"Are you laughing?"

"Nora, you are so gullible." She slapped the counter and wheezed. "I can't catch my breath."

Her laughter verged on hysteria. I was not amused. "You're a butthead," I informed her with a raised brow.

"I never said I was pregnant," Gilly answered. "But your assumption is hilarious. You should have seen your face." Her whole body shook with laughter and she literally slapped her knee. "Priceless."

I rolled my eyes. "Fine, fine." I put down the Windex bottle. "Why do you need my support?"

She straightened, suddenly sobered, and with calm measure, she declared, "I've decided to grow out the gray in my hair."

Nooooooo! This was far worse than a *whoops baby* in my book. I took a few slow, deep breaths, then summoned my strength. "That's so amazingly great." I stared at her chestnut-brown hair. It was pulled back into a braid, which was the way she liked to wear it when she worked. I could see the rich brown of her hairline, which meant she'd colored it recently. "I'm here for you. Totally," I added.

"It's a good thing you don't make a living as a spy, because you're saying one thing, but your face," she circled her finger at me, "is telling me a whole 'nother story."

The idea of watching Gilly grow gray was like watching my own mortality. I wasn't sure I was ready for it. "When did you decide this?"

"Been thinking about it for a while now. The gray is growing out faster than every six weeks. I have to do touch-ups at home every couple of weeks now in between trips to the salon."

"I do my own color. It's not that big of a deal. I can teach you."

She placed her hands on her rounded hips. "I'm going gray, Nora, and that's the end of this conversation."

I winced. "It's your life."

It was Gilly's turn to roll her eyes. "It's my hair, not my life."

I raised my brows but left it at that. "Can you believe Pippa is learning how to drive a motorcycle?" I asked, changing the subject.

"She's going to break her flippin' neck!" Gilly exclaimed. Gilly had been ranting about Pippa's decision for a week now, so I knew the redirection would work. "Just because her biker barista rides, doesn't mean she has to do it. I mean, she's younger than us, but she's still no spring chicken."

I looked around as if our thirty-something friend

3

might overhear Gilly's complaints even though I knew Pippa was spending time with her guy on this lovely Wednesday afternoon. This was her only chance for time off, considering we were two days away from Memorial Day weekend, one of the biggest tourism weekends of the year.

"Pippa will be fine," I reassured Gilly, even though I wasn't exactly convinced myself.

"I wish you had futuristic visions, instead of seeing past memories. I'd feel a lot safer knowing that Pippa would be safe on that crotch rocket."

"There are no guarantees in life," I said. "And the only way to stop Pippa from riding a motorcycle is to hog-tie her then lock her in your basement until the end of time."

"Works for me," muttered Gilly. "When's the last time you smelled her?"

Oh for the love of Pete's pits. I'd had enough of being forced to sniff my friends. After dying for twenty-seven seconds during my hysterectomy, I'd woken up with a nose that could literally smell trouble. At least if that trouble was contained in the memories of other people. It seemed to work as long as the odor evoked strong emotions, so the visions weren't all bad, thank heavens.

The first several weeks after finding out about my new smell-o-vision gift, Gilly and Pippa had constantly made me smell them—like, all day, every day—to test my ability. As a result, I now knew way more about my two closest gal pals than I wanted to or should. I was so happy when the shiny newness of my ability finally wore off, and they stopped shoving their wrists under my nose.

"Jordy will make sure she's safe," I said.

I'd given Jordy Hines, the tattooed owner of Moo-La-Lattes and Pippa's new beau, a lecture about Pippa wearing a helmet and pads at all times that served as a not-so thinly veiled threat. Pippa was like our younger sister. And we followed the sibling rule: We were allowed to torture her, but we'd junk-punch anyone else who hurt her.

"Are we still on for dinner tonight?" Gilly asked.

"Of course, we are."

My BFF had been a little lost this past week, because her ex-husband, Giovanni Rossi, had called a few weeks back and asked if the teen twins could fly out to Vegas to spend time with him. She'd never spent more than a night or two away from her dynamic duo, and their absence was taking its toll. Next summer, the twins would graduate high school and go off to college. I couldn't imagine what Gilly would be like without her children around for months at a time. It would probably feel like getting fired from motherhood.

I'd made a standing date with her for every day the kids were gone, and since they still had one more day in Vegas, I was Gilly's for the night. She needed the company, and in all fairness, she'd done as much or more for me, especially when I'd dealt with the last harrowing months of my mother's terminal cancer. Gilly had been a rock for me, offering a safe space to break down when I felt overwhelmed.

Gilly walked past me and gave me a hip bump. "I feel bad keeping you from Detective Hottie."

"Ezra's been busy with work and such," I said. The "and such" was actually Ezra's teenaged son, Mason. The sixteen-year-old boy was staying with him while Ezra's ex-wife, Kati Portman, and her resort-owner husband went on a two-week vacation to the Bahamas. Ezra hadn't introduced me to his son yet, but also, I hadn't asked for an introduction.

I'd never had kids. Being the godmother of Gilly's teens was the closest I'd ever gotten to motherhood. And I was happy with my choice not to have had children. Still, a part of me would have liked Ezra to, at least, *want* me to meet his kid. I mean, while we hadn't exactly defined our relationship, we were more than just mattress buddies.

"Is there trouble in paradise?" Gilly teased. When I didn't answer right away, Gilly narrowed her gaze. "You know I'm not serious, right? Are things okay between you and Easy?" Easy was Ezra's nickname, used by co-workers and friends. I called him Ezra, but I wasn't above teasing Mr. Easy Like Sunday Morning.

"Ezra and I are awesome," I said, not wanting to delve too deeply into what might or might not be going on between Ezra and me. "Like I said, he's been busy, is all. You know how it is with kids around."

"Oh, that's right. He has his son. For how much longer?"

"Until next weekend."

"I still can't believe Big Don let Roger go away over Memorial weekend."

Donald Portman owned Portman's on the Lake, one of the big five resorts in Garden Cove. His son Roger managed the place for him, and eight years ago, Roger married Ezra's ex-wife, Kati. Ezra had relocated to the area to be closer to Mason. I hadn't been around then; my career had taken me to Chicago. But I'd grown up with Roger. He was a year older than Gilly and me, and he'd always been a showboat.

"I can't believe Big Don let Roger go on vacation at all, much less during the busiest tourist weekend of the year." I shrugged. "Maybe the old coot was feeling generous."

"Hah!" Gilly clucked her tongue. "Big Don doesn't have a generous bone in his body. And believe me, I know. The man wagged his ungenerous bone at me once when he'd stopped in for a massage at the Rose Palace."

I swallowed back a gag. "That's disgusting."

"I wish he was the worst person I'd ever run into at the Rose Palace."

Until recently, Gilly had been the spa manager at the Rose Palace Resort. That is, until Phil Williams, the jackhole who ran the resort, had fired her after she'd gotten arrested for a murder she didn't commit. Phil had been up to his filthy eyeballs in the death of Gilly's ex-boyfriend, Lloyd Briscoll. Unfortunately, the only person who could connect Phil to Lloyd's murder was the actual killer, Carl Grigsby, a dirty cop on Phil's payroll. He told me about Phil right before shooting me. The bullet had ripped through my leg, and I hadn't given him another chance to aim better.

I beat him into a coma. My ex-husband, Shawn, who

happened to be the chief of police, had ordered police protection around the clock for the time being, just in case Phil got it in his head to take out the only witness to his connection to Lloyd.

Sometimes, I went to the hospital to sit with him. I'm not sure why. I didn't feel guilty for knocking his head in. It was him or me. Carl Grigsby had totally deserved it. But it wasn't justice. He needed to wake up so he could face the consequences of his actions, for the arsons, the murder, and for shooting me.

"I'm glad you're working here now," I told her. "With me." I put my arm around her shoulder. "And you no longer have to deal with lecherous men looking for happy endings."

Gilly laughed. "That's the God's truth." She put away the last of the cleaning supplies in the utility closet. "Let's get out of here."

After turning off the lights, turning on the alarm, and locking the door, we separated on the sidewalk. Since early-bird tourists were already in Garden Cove, parking spaces were scarce. Gilly had parked two blocks down in a public lot on the other side of Dolly's Dollhouse Emporium, but I'd gotten to work early enough to get a space one block over near the courthouse.

I smiled when I saw a familiar face coming up the sidewalk. "Reese, how nice to see you." Reese McKay, a young patrol officer, had been one of the cops on the scene the night I'd been shot. As a matter of fact, she'd been Carl Grigsby's unlucky partner. No one had been more shocked about Carl's seedy side than her.

She smiled back and waved. "Hey, Nora. Nice day, huh?" She looked up at the clear blue sky and shielded her eyes from the sun before pivoting her gaze back to me. "I hope this keeps up for the weekend."

"Same," I replied. I dug my keys from my purse. "It's going to be a busy weekend."

"Tell me about it." She sighed. "I don't know who's worse, the drunk and rowdy tourists stirring up trouble or the small-time crooks in Garden Cove trying to rip them off. It's a nightmare."

She wore a pair of jeans and a butter-yellow tank top. Her strawberry-blonde hair was down around her shoulders, and the wind kept whipping strands about her face.

I jangled my keys. "I don't want to keep you from your errands."

Reese snorted as she pushed the offending hair away, and she looked back toward the courthouse. "I wish you were interrupting errands."

"Is something wrong?"

"Always," she said. "At least where my cousin Fiona is concerned. She had a court appearance this afternoon."

Since Reese had instigated the information, I didn't feel too much like a nosy Parker when I asked, "Anything serious?"

"Damn girl ran a red light then blew a point-one-five on the breathalyzer. This one was two and half months ago. It's her second DUI in the past twelve months."

"That's not good."

"Tell me about it."

"Where's she at now? Did they lock her up or something?" A blood alcohol over point-one-five carried a minimum jail time, along with fines and license suspension. I only knew this because my dad, God rest his soul, used to be Garden Cove's police chief. Now, my ex-husband, Shawn Rafferty, was the guy in charge.

"Nothing like that, though she'd probably be better off facing some real consequences. The prosecutor is an old friend of my uncle Reagan. Reagan owns half the commercial real estate here in town, so the prosecutor cut Fiona a break. She's paying the fine right now, and her license has been suspended for a year, plus she has to attend AA meetings."

"Sounds like she could use the meetings."

"You don't get sober just because a judge orders it." I detected the bitter tone of experience in her words. "I'll believe it when I see it."

"Well, hopefully this is a wake-up call for her."

A young woman with thick auburn hair and a body that rivaled J-Lo's, including the curvy booty, trotted up behind Reese. "Hey, Cuz," she said. "Ready to go?"

Reese rolled her eyes. "Yep." She nodded toward me. "Nora Black, this is my cousin, Fiona McKay."

Her eyes widened with delight. "Nora Black of Scents and Scentsability?"

"One and the same," I replied.

Fiona scooted around Reese, threw open her arms and hugged me. She had a wide, gold-toned cuff bracelet on her left wrist, and it dug into my back.

"It's so nice to meet you," she gushed. "I love your

lotions." She held her bangle-free wrist up to my face. "I'm wearing your blond sandalwood and rosemary lotion right now. God, it's yummy."

It *was* yummy.

It also triggered a vision.

"Come on, sugar," Fiona said. Like all my scent-induced visions, I couldn't see her face, but her voice, her hair, and her body made it quite evident this was her memory. "You promised to give me a taste."

A tall, thin man wearing a western shirt, a bolo tie, jeans that bagged a little, and pointy-toed, red and black cowboy boots, leaned his fuzzed-out face into hers. I heard some disgusting smacking of lips and tongues.

After they finished kissing, the guy said, "I can't deny you anything, dumpling." He reached into his pocket and pulled out a small vial of white powder. "I got your candy right here."

He opened the top and dabbed the drugs onto the meaty part of Fiona's hand. I caught a glimpse of a watch with a dark face and some gold lines.

"Are you all right?" Fiona asked, alarmed. "Hello? Reese's Pieces, I think there's something wrong with your friend."

Reese stared at me expectantly. "Did you just...?"

I nodded. She was aware of my scratch-n-sniff psychic ability to tap into other people's memories. I tried to convey my horror at what I'd seen, but Reese shook her head. "Forget it. I don't want to know."

"What?" asked Fiona, frowning as she looked from me to her cousin. "What are you guys talking about?"

"Nothing," said Reese. "See you later, Nora." She

grabbed her cousin by the arm and hauled her down the sidewalk and away from me.

Reese hadn't wanted to know about the memory. Was it because she suspected her cousin was into more than booze? My heart broke a little for the both of them.

CHAPTER 2

*W*hen I pulled into my driveway, I saw a familiar red truck parked on the street about six feet from my mailbox. My heart sped up as I turned off my car, undid my seat belt and got out. I met the green-eyed gaze of Ezra Holden, aka Detective Hottie. He stood on my porch wearing a black muscle-cut t-shirt, and damn, if it didn't hug his wide chest and his large biceps in a way that made my nonexistent ovaries weep.

His jeans were a no-nonsense straight leg, relaxed fit. He wasn't the kind of man who wore skinny jeans. Thank God. He crossed his arms and watched me put my keys in my purse before walking toward him. Considering he hadn't contacted me other than to text me some kind of bizarre dinner menu, I was surprised he'd shown up on my doorstep. And wow, did he look good. In fact, I was *this close* to changing my mind about him shimmying on a pair of skinny jeans. "What are you doing here?" I asked.

"Don't tell me the romance is dead already," he said, half-jest, half-serious. "I hoped you'd be glad to see me."

"Of course, I'm glad to see you." I glanced around. "But...I thought we were cooling it while your kid was staying with you."

"What? I never said that," Ezra replied. His lashes, several shades darker than his sandy-brown hair, lowered at me.

I recognized disappointment when I saw it. "I don't know what to think. It's been a week," I told him. "You haven't called or come by, and you only texted me once." I shrugged. "And it wasn't like I was going to bring over a lollipop, eggplant, tacos, and fireworks. I'm not a grocery delivery service."

He stared at me. "Nora, sweetheart, I was sexting you."

"What?" My eyes widened, and Ezra cracked his first smile since my arrival.

"You know, sex plus text equals sext."

"I'm not that old. I know what sexting is." I laughed. "But next time you should use your words, because I thought you were sending me meal suggestions."

He chuckled. "I was," he said, his voice low. "Only *you* were the intended meal."

I felt heat rush to my cheeks. "How is a lollipop sexting? I mean, I get the eggplant." I smirked. "And the taco. But a lollipop?"

He pulled me into his arms and gave me a kiss that made my scalp buzz. "It means," he said as he pulled back, "I want to lick you all over."

"Oh." I blinked as my body reacted to his words. "Oh boy. Uhm, are you planning on coming in?"

"I can't," he said. "Like you said, it's been a week, and I wanted to see you. Even if it was only for five minutes." He sighed as he pressed his forehead to mine. "I've got to get home. I promised Mason I'd watch the game with him tonight."

"Next time call me. Or regular text me, and I'll make sure I get off a little early."

"And then we'll both get off."

I smacked his chest. "Just not too early."

He grinned. "I'd love to take this conversation to a satisfying conclusion, but the baseball game starts in thirty minutes, and, speaking of tacos, I have to pick some up on the way home from the Taco Shake Shack for Mason and me. I can't be late for the game. This is the first time I've had him for this long, and I don't want to blow it with the boy."

I smiled, hiding my disappointment. "I get it. Kid trumps...uh, me." I almost said girlfriend, but we hadn't exactly gotten to the define-the-relationship stage. We'd been seeing each other regularly for a few months. But Ezra and I weren't flaunting the fact that we were dating. And by dating, I meant Ezra cooking dinner for me at my place before we watched a movie. Or went upstairs for mind- and body-bending sex. We rarely went out. I wasn't sure if that was Ezra's doing or my own.

His phone beeped. "That'll be Mason," he said on a sigh.

"At least you're having fun, right?" I asked. "Lots of dad-son bonding and all that good stuff."

"Most of the time. He likes to push it sometimes, but he's a good kid."

"With you for a dad, I'm sure he is." I was rewarded with another kiss. "He's probably easy-peasy," I said, using Ezra's nickname as a way to tease him.

He gave me a half smile. "I don't know," he said. "Would you maybe want to meet him?"

Cripes. Meeting the son. That was a big step. And yeah, okay, I'd been thinking about how Ezra hadn't invited me to meet Mason. But now that he had, I was instantly worried. What would Mason think of me? Would he think I was...*gulp*...too old for his dad?

"Sure," I finally replied, not sure at all. "Set it up."

"Really?" The relief in his voice didn't bring me any comfort. "I figured since you don't want children...I don't want to scare you off by moving too fast."

"Just because I don't want kids of my own doesn't mean I avoid other people's children." What did he mean, moving too fast for what? It wasn't like I was in any danger of becoming the boy's stepmother. I had no intention of marrying anyone ever again. I liked being happily un-wed. "Besides, teenagers are better than toddlers."

"Oh really?"

"Well, yeah. They can practically take care of themselves. I'm in no danger of changing diapers or singing annoying songs about buses or baby sharks."

Ezra laughed. "That's fair." His phone beeped again. "I better get going." He let go of me and stepped back.

"If you decide you want to try that sexting thing again, maybe use actual words," I said. "The eggplant is funny, but the taco is gross. What were the fireworks for?"

"The orgasm I plan to give you."

I grinned. "You are *very* good at generating fireworks."

He backed me up against the front door, his voice low and growly. "Keep talking like that and Mason will be watching the game on his own." And then he kissed me stupid.

* * *

Mason did not watch the game on his own, because like the good person I am, I sent Ezra home to his son. I had jumped in the shower to get ready for dinner with Gilly and was drying my hair when my phone chimed out a notification. I didn't want to mess up another sexting session with Ezra, so I reached for my reading glasses on the end of the vanity and knocked them into the trash bin.

"Damn it!" Luckily, they'd landed on top, but I had to wash them, dry them, and find the lens-cleaning cloth before I could put them on and see the words. I unlocked the screen with the fingerprint scanner on the back.

The text was from Gilly, not Ezra. I opened it up.

I need you, the text said. *Gio is on his way here with the twins.*

I texted her back. *He sent the twins home early? What a*

17

jerk. I re-read her text and let out a shocked breath. Then I added: *Gio is in Missouri?*

Yes. He rented a car at the airport. They'll be here soon.

Holy freaking crap, Gilly.

Right?! I need backup, STAT.

Gio had been toxic for Gilly. She'd been nearly ruined when he'd decided to dump their marriage and their kids to run off to Vegas for the career he could never have in Garden Cove. Gilly had offered to move with him if it would save their relationship, but Gio wanted out of the full-time husband-and-dad gig. In other words, he was a good-for-nothing dickbag.

I'm on my way, BFF. Remember, I always keep a shovel and garbage bags in my trunk.

LOL. Thank you. <3 <3 <3 <3 <3 I can always count on you.

CHAPTER 3

Gilly lived in a two-story home on a cul-de-sac near two others, though the one on the left now sat empty with a For Sale sign in its yard. The owner, Mr. Garner, had nearly gotten Gilly put in jail for murder after he'd stabbed her abusive ex-boyfriend, Lloyd Briscoll. Granted, he had a good reason—Lloyd had strangled his daughter to death.

It turned out while Mr. Garner had stabbed Lloyd in the stomach, he hadn't actually murdered the louse. So, the old man had taken a plea deal, and spent four weeks in jail for assault with a deadly weapon and obstruction of justice. After he was released, he and his dog Godiva moved to Santa Rosa, New Mexico, to be near his sister. I didn't blame him. Garden Cove had offered him nothing but heartbreak.

Gilly opened the front door wearing a black body-contouring dress that showed off her every curve, and she'd put on full makeup, including fake eyelashes and coral lipstick that complimented her skin tone and her dark eyes. Her chestnut-brown hair had a fresh, glowing aura about it and not a gray hair in sight. I guess her threat to go gray had been squashed by L'Oreal.

"I will not let that bastard see me frumpy and haggard, Nora," she said. "I won't do it."

"You've never looked frumpy, honey. Not even on a bad day. Right now, you look va-va-voom. Gio will swallow his tongue when he sees you."

The pinched look around her eyes relaxed. A slight smile turned up the corners of her perfectly painted lips. "Thanks. I needed to hear that." She swallowed hard and shook her head. "What the hell is he thinking coming here? What does he want?" Her worried stare met mine. "You know he wants something. He never does anything nice without expecting something in return."

Yeah. Her ex was all kinds of selfish. Giovanni Rossi had been the head chef at the Rose Palace Resort until he got his dream gig in Las Vegas. He'd taken the job then asked for a divorce because he wanted a fresh start without his wife and two small children.

Even ten years later, I got pissed off about what he'd done. I never spoke ill of the jerk in front of the twins because Gilly wanted it that way, but I hated him. What he did to Gilly, up and leaving like he did, made him a monster in my book. I would never forgive him.

Instead of sitting on the couch, Gilly stationed herself by the front window. I shut the door behind me, put my purse down on the bottom step of the stairway leading to the second floor, then joined her.

"This is your home, Gilly. Bought and paid for by

you without any help from Gio. You can tell him to get right back into his rental car, turn around, and keep driving until he hits the Pacific. And drowns."

"He's their father, Nora," she said, miserable. "Whatever he did to me, I can't let that effect my kids."

"He abandoned all of you," I told her. "You've been both mom and dad to Marco and Ari for the past ten years. Gio has been a father in name, sperm, and blood only, not where or when it counts."

She sighed. "Tell that to Marco. He couldn't stop going on and on about how much fun he and his dad had riding the roller coaster at the top of the Stratosphere. I haven't heard him that animated or happy in years, Nora. Years."

"He's almost seventeen years old, Gils. And you're the one person in his life that he knows will love him no matter his mood." I hugged her. "He trusts that he can show you every part of him, and you're not going to disappear. Gio will never be able to say that."

Gilly patted my back. "You're right. But all the 'Dad this' and 'Dad that' has gotten under my skin, you know?"

I let her go and stepped back. "I do know. Gio waltzes back into their lives after ten years and you have to pretend it doesn't rip your heart out." I didn't mention that if Gio stayed true to form, he'd hurt my godchildren all over again. I already knew Gilly had that fear. But what was she supposed to do? Life wasn't always easy. I imagined the hardest lesson a parent had to impart to their children was how to deal with pain. Hadn't I dealt with that lesson at the age of fifty, watching my mother waste away with brain cancer?

"Gio is your past, but he'll always be a part of your life because of the kids." I gave her a sympathetic look. "How long before he gets here?"

"Ari texted me right before you got here." She rubbed her upper arms as if warding off a chill. "So, any minute."

On cue, headlights shone their way up her street, a glowing beam swiping across her gauzy, champagne-colored curtains.

Gilly grabbed my hand, squeezing hard enough to make me wince. "That's them," she said.

I watched as Gio the jackhole got out of a red mini SUV. I groaned inwardly when I noticed he was wearing slim, tapered black dress pants—the dressy version of skinny jeans—and a tight black, short-sleeved polo shirt. Worse, he still had all his hair, even if it was more silver than black now.

"Oh, God, Nora. He still looks delicious."

"He looks like a turd squeezed into a black sausage casing," I said.

She snorted. "Liar."

I shrugged. "It's what I see." And it wasn't a complete lie. To me, Gio would always look like something that should be flushed twice. I took a deep breath to calm myself for the sake of my godchildren. They didn't need to see Aunt Nora lose her mind over their dad. Frankly, he was lucky I'd left my gun at home.

Gio opened the SUV's back door and Ari scooted out, her duffel bag over her shoulder and her arms crossed over her chest. Marco might have been happy to spend time with his father, but Ari looked like she'd spent her entire vacation sucking lemons. Poor kid. Maybe she'd seen her father for what he really was...a narcissistic liar.

Gilly nudged me with her elbow. "They're coming. Move." She pushed me away from the window. "Move!" she said more urgently. "I don't want them to think I'm anxiously waiting."

"I'll run Gio over with my car. Just say the word."

"Maybe wait for the kids to go to bed first," she said with a weak smile.

I chuckled and brushed her shoulder with mine. "Good plan."

The door handle rattled.

Gilly grimaced.

The door opened. Ari walked in, slid her duffel bag across the floor, then hurried across the living room and threw her arms around her mom's neck. Gilly appeared startled for a moment, then she closed her eyes and hugged her daughter back.

Abruptly, Ari disengaged. She cast a look back at her brother then raced up the stairs two at a time.

Gilly raised her brow at her son. Marco shrugged. He kissed his mom on the cheek then smiled at me. "Hey, Aunt Nora."

Well, at least I wasn't invisible. "Hey, kiddo." I raised my hand. He high-fived me then headed up after his twin.

My expression soured as I took in the Italian piece of crap in the doorway smiling at my best friend.

"Hello, Gillian," he said in a slightly accented voice. "You look beautiful."

Gilly's eyes narrowed. "You can drop the fake charm, Gio." Her frown deepened. "It doesn't work on me anymore."

He shrugged and raised his hands palms up. "I don't want to fight."

The words were reasonable, but I knew they were meant to make Gilly defensive. "Yeah, right," I muttered under my breath.

"Nora." His lip curled into a snarl. "Is there a reason you're here?"

Tension filled my body, but Gilly squeezed my shoulder. I couldn't relax, but I pressed my lips together to prevent the insults from spilling out of my mouth.

"Nora was invited," said Gilly. "You were not. Why did you come back with the kids?"

"I've decided to come home."

Shock rooted me to the floor. I glanced at my BFF and saw her expression reflected exactly what I felt. Wasn't that like Gio? Drop a bombshell just to see what would blow up.

"The hell you say," said Gilly. "This isn't your home."

"I mean, Garden Cove," Gio said. "I've taken a head chef position at Players Restaurant at Portman's on the Lake."

"Why?" I blurted.

"Not that it's any of your business, Nora, but I took the position because I miss my family."

"Wow. It only took a whole decade for you to miss

your family." I snorted my disbelief and shook my head. "Bullshit."

"You can believe what you want," he said, pressing both hands against his chest. He had the audacity to look sincere. "I know my heart."

"You don't have a heart," I snapped.

Gio wasn't smooth enough to stop the flash of anger in his brown eyes, but he quickly covered his irritation.

A door slammed upstairs.

Gilly sighed. "I guess you told the kids already."

"I told Marco and Ariana last night."

"Ari," Gilly corrected. "She likes to be called Ari."

"That's not her name," Gio said.

My eyes widened. No wonder Ari had looked pissed. She hated being called Ariana.

"Ari *is* our daughter's name," said Gilly. "You'd know that if you'd bothered to stay in regular contact."

"The past is the past," said Gio, carelessly waving a hand as though doing so made the last ten years of his negligence disappear. "I'm staying at Portman's on the Lake."

"What? No room left in Hell?" I questioned. Gilly grasped my forearm and squeezed. I nearly had to swallow my tongue to keep from reading Gio the riot act. He wasn't my ex. And I knew I had to let Gilly fight her own battles.

For now.

Gio ignored me. "I'm only living at Portman's until I find a suitable house."

"You're serious," said Gilly. "You really are returning to Garden Cove."

"I'm not going anywhere," he said, pointing his judgmental gaze at my BFF. "I'm not going to leave my family again. That includes you, Gilly."

"No, it doesn't," she said, her voice trembling.

"Gilly..." He stepped forward as though he might take her hand.

I placed myself between him and my BFF. I hoped to get some strong scent-memory that could clue me in on Gio's true motives for returning, but the woodsy cologne he wore offered me zero insight.

"I've got this, Nora," Gilly said, as she gently ushered me aside. She gave her ex an assessing glance. "If you want to be a part of Marco and Ari's life, I'm great with that. Though, I will tell you, they're sixteen, almost seventeen, and frankly, they don't need a lot of parenting anymore. However, if you have any idea of reclaiming a life with me, I'll tell you right now, that is completely off the table."

"Are you seeing someone?"

Typical Gio. He didn't hear Gilly say "no." He heard, "if you play your cards right, you might have a shot."

"If I was, that would be none of your business." She pointed her finger back and forth between the two of them. "We're divorced. Remember?"

He pursed his lips, his eyes darting around as if trying to think of the appropriate comeback. It must have escaped him, because he simply gave Gilly a curt nod. "We'll talk more when I get settled."

"As long as it's about the kids," Gilly reiterated.

Gio turned on his expensive Italian loafer and

headed back to the car. I jumped at the door handle and slammed it shut.

Gilly walked to the window, standing with her arms crossed as she watched the man who'd wrecked her life pull out of the driveway. When his car disappeared from sight, her shoulders sagged.

"I can't stand that he still looks so good," she said. "Still handsome."

"Yeah, and so was Ted Bundy," I added.

Gilly nodded, but she didn't say anything.

I put my arm around her shoulder. "Don't get twisted about him, Gils. He's not worth it."

"Did you get some kind of vision?" she asked. "We both know there has to be another reason he's really moving back here."

I shook my head. "I tried. Nothing."

She nodded again then patted my hand. "I better go check on the twins."

"Good idea." Crap on a cracker. I swore to all that was unholy, if Giovanni Rossi screwed with Gilly, I was going to find a way to make him disappear. As a cop's daughter, I was not without ideas.

My phone played "Bad Boys" and I jerked to attention. "That's Ezra," I said.

"Go answer it." Gilly gently urged me toward my purse when the chorus sang out again. "Go."

It took only a second of digging for me to find my phone. I hit the connect button right as the chorus started for a third time. "Hey," I said as I put it to my ear.

27

"Hey, Nora," Ezra said. He sounded cautious. Worried.

"Is anything the matter?"

"Do you want to go to dinner with Mason and me tomorrow night?"

"Uhm." I blinked. Rapidly. We'd discussed the possibility of me meeting his kid, but I guess I hadn't expected it to be this soon.

Snap out of it, I told myself. It's not like he'd confessed his undying love for me. It was dinner. With his son. Was I ready? It was a big step, and it could add complications to our relationship that we'd avoided by staying in a romantic and sexy bubble.

"It's okay if you don't want to," he said.

"No, no," I lied. "It's not that. I'm at Gilly's. Her ex-husband just flew in from Vegas with the kids, and he dropped a bomb on Gilly that he's moving back to Garden Cove."

"Wow," Ezra said. "That *is* a bomb."

"Right?" Some of the tension I held eased.

"So, are we on for dinner?"

The tension choked me like a zip tie. "Oh, uhm."

"It's fine, Nora. We can do it another time. Or never. It's up to you." He sounded disappointed, and I felt my heart squeeze. What was wrong with me? I was meeting his kid, not going to my execution.

"Ezra, I'd love to go to dinner with you and Mason."

He said nothing for a moment, then asked, "Are you sure?"

"Yes," I said.

"Okay. Good. See you tomorrow."

"Looking forward to it." I ended the call as Gilly came back down the stairs. "Are the kids okay?"

"Depends on your definition of okay, but yes. They'll be fine."

"Gio's an ass," I muttered, unable to keep it in.

"Tell me something I don't know," Gilly said on a sigh and then changed the subject. "How are things going with Detective Hottie?"

"Fast," I said. "I'm meeting his son tomorrow night."

CHAPTER 4

*T*he next day, I awoke with the sniffles and a feeling of trepidation as I got myself ready for work. The doctor had prescribed an allergy pill and a nasal spray, but I'd only been taking the pill the last few weeks because my seasonal allergies hadn't been all that bad. I couldn't find the nasal spray, so I decided I'd have to rely on the pill to stop Mother Nature's snotty attack.

The sun was shining, the temperature was seventy-six degrees, and the songbirds were chirping. I rolled the car window down to enjoy the beautiful weather.

A big mistake. My eyes and throat began to itch.

I sneezed.

Crap.

Mother Nature was a bitch.

I resisted the urge to rub my eyes because I was just vain enough to want to avoid racoon eyes before I'd even gotten to work. I had to park by the courthouse again, and on my walk to the shop, my nose dripped, two hard sneezes nearly blew out my itchy eyeballs, and my gummy vision failed me. I tripped over a broken piece of concrete and nearly landed face-first on the sidewalk. I managed to maintain my balance, but my big toe throbbed and my knees ached.

When I walked into Scents & Scentsability, Pippa Davenport, my friend and employee, was setting up a display table. She wore a diaphanous pale blue, long-sleeved chiffon blouse over an egg-shell camisole, along with a pair of chocolate-brown palazzo pants that flattered her willowy frame.

Pippa took one look at me and scooted out from behind the counter. "Cripes almighty, Nora," she said. "Have you been crying?"

"No," I said nasally.

She leaned back. "Are you sick? Is it contagious?"

I shook my head. "Allergies. I swear the pollen fairy visited and dumped a ton of it on my head."

"Have you been taking your meds?"

"I'm taking my Claritin daily."

Pippa had a habit of trying to mommy me—a side effect of our previous working relationship when she was my assistant. Back when I was a corporate drone, I relied on her to keep my schedule, both personal and professional, on track. I never worried about her constant mothering because that's what assistants did. These days, however, it sometimes felt like Pippa fussed over me because she thought I was getting too old to take care of myself. Like fifty-one was old. Hah.

"Maybe you need a decongestant," she suggested.

"I need you to stop worrying about me. I've

31

managed to treat my allergies without anyone's help for twenty-odd years, Pip."

Her brow furrowed as she met my gaze. "First, I'm your friend, and I'm never going to stop worrying about you. And second, you used to always ask me to go get your allergy meds when I worked as your assistant, so don't give me any crap about managing without help."

I sneezed and my ears popped, prompting me to give up the fight. "Fine. You win. I'll get some decongestants and eye drops when the pharmacy opens," I promised. It was seven-thirty. The pharmacy wouldn't open until eight.

"Let me take your mind off your allergies," she said. "Guess what I heard yesterday?"

I chuckled then sniffed. "Aliens have landed? Big Foot is running amok? Someone spotted Nessy in the lake?"

"Next time, consider my question rhetorical." Pippa, a lifelong big-city girl, had gotten on board with the small-town gossip grapevine. She was aces at eavesdropping, and so was her boyfriend, Jordy, the owner of Moo-La-Lattes.

"Soooo, what did you hear?"

"I probably shouldn't say anything, but since it involves you..."

"Me?" Maybe my relationship with Ezra was making its way around the gossip circles. Did I care? Maybe? I didn't know. "Just give it up."

Pippa looked giddy. "I heard Roger Portman took his wife out of town to work on their marriage.

According to the rumor mill, Roger was having an affair with a waitress at the resort."

I widened my eyes, then blinked rapidly as tears blurred my vision. Well, that was news. And it was also a good reason why Big Don might allow his son and daughter-in-law to take off to the Bahamas.

"Are you crying?"

"No," I said flatly. "I'm itchy. I'd like to scratch out my eyeballs." I clenched my fingers and forced my hands to stay by my side. "Flippin' allergies," I growled.

"Yeah. Um, okay." She patted my shoulder. "It's not like Ezra would dump you to take up with his ex-wife again."

I blinked at her some more, but this time, the cause was shock in addition to allergies. "Gee. Thanks."

"And if Roger and Kati get divorced, she and Mason probably wouldn't move away from Garden Cove, right?"

I could see that Pippa had done a little too much thinking about the situation. I had barely made the decision to meet Ezra's son, and now Pippa was speculating about his possible departure.

"Would you stop trying to reassure me?" I asked. "I don't know anything about this stupid rumor. I haven't seen Roger, other than by accident, in a long time. I have no idea if he would cheat on his wife or not."

"But Ezra would know, right? Because he's got Mason while his ex is trying to work out things with Roger."

"You don't know that." But trying to fix marriage problems made more sense as to why Roger took a vacation during the town's busiest weekend of the year. Had Big Don forced him to go? I shook my head. I couldn't see Roger's dad caring one way or the other what his golden boy got up to.

Was this something I mentioned to Ezra? If I did, would he think I was a busybody? Probably. But...if he had known but didn't tell me, what did that mean? Either it wasn't my business, or he hadn't told me because...well, no use going through the door Pippa opened.

I sighed.

He was taking care of his son while his ex was out of town. She might have told him, and it wasn't like there was any reason for him to share the information with me. "What's the name of Roger's side piece?"

"Sorry," Pip said. "The mysterious mistress was not named."

"Well, I hope it's not true. I don't wish ill on Ezra's ex." My nose started to drip. I frantically dug in my purse, trying to find some tissue as the tell-tale tickle caused two short and sharp intakes of breath.

Then I sneezed again. "Oh, gawd."

Pippa, who had the grace and reaction time of a hummingbird, jumped out of the way. She pointed to the door. "Go now, Nora. Wait in the parking lot until the place opens."

Under her chiffon sleeve, I saw a huge red scrape that stretched the length of her forearm.

"Fine," I said, knowing I sounded every bit as grumpy as I felt. I had to get this allergy attack under control. I couldn't show up to meet Ezra's son looking like I had a severe case of pink eye. "I'll go. But when I get back, we're going to talk about the road rash on your arm."

* * *

CRAYMORE'S PHARMACY was a few blocks from the shop. Since parking was so hard to find, I decided to walk. By the time I got there, my symptoms were worse. Well, what did I expect? I traded allergy relief for a good parking space.

I leaned against the brick wall of the pharmacy, put in my earbuds, and started the audiobook app on my phone. I spent twenty minutes listening and using up the few tissues I'd shoved in my purse. Gah. So much for Claritin's magic allergy repellant. I wished I'd been able to find the nasal spray. I hadn't been this stuffed up in a while.

When a young man in a Craymore's apron finally opened the front door, I wanted to hug him.

The only decongestant that had ever really worked for me was an antihistamine-pseudoephedrine combo called Pseudo-Act. It was awesome. It also had one of the main ingredients in meth. Thanks to the prevalence of meth producers in the Midwest, I had to jump through a dozen fiery hoops to purchase it.

The pharmacy tech was a middle-aged woman with dark brown skin. She wore a white jacket with the name *Barb* embroidered on the right side above a breast pocket. She forced a smile when I sidled up to the counter. Huh. Maybe she didn't like early-bird customers.

Well, I didn't like my head feeling like a balloon filled with concrete.

"Can I help you?" she asked, her tone just short of curt.

"I need some Pseudo-Act." I pointed to the red box on the shelf full of different brands of decongestants.

She eyed me suspiciously. "For what purpose?"

I bit my tongue to keep from making a *Breaking Bad* reference. Instead, I blinked, gummy tears sticking to my lashes, and sneezed. I grabbed a tissue from the box near the register. "Allergies," I said, as if it weren't obvious.

"Driver's license," she ordered.

"You got it." I dug my wallet out of my purse. "Here it is." I flipped it open to show my ID behind a clear plastic sleeve

"Take it out, please." Her lips were tight with disapproval.

I fumbled around for a few moments, trying and failing to retrieve it. "Why do they make these slots childproof?"

"Here, let me help," someone said from behind me.

I turned to see Leila Rafferty, my ex-husband's wife. Leila had been in treatment for Non-Hodgkin's lymphoma for the past six or seven months. I'd given her my mother's lace-front wigs in March, and it made me happy to see her wearing the dark blonde wavy bob with honey highlights. She smiled at me and held up a pair of tweezers.

"Hi there." I smiled back, happily turning over my wallet. "It's so nice to see you."

"You sound hoarse," she said. "Are you getting a cold?"

"Nothing like that," I told her. "Just too much pollen in the air."

"The news said the pollen index was through the roof today. They're predicting it will last for a few days."

"Awesome."

Leila used the tweezers to grip my driver's license and slid it out. "Voila," she said with a fair amount of triumph.

"Neat trick," I told her.

"I can never get my ID out of my billfold. Necessity is the mother of invention."

"Isn't that the truth." I handed my driver's license to the surly pharm tech then turned back to Leila. "How have you been?"

"Not too bad," she replied. "I haven't had any chemotherapy in a month, so I've gotten a bit of my appetite back."

Impulsively, I reached out and squeezed her hand. "That's great."

"Yeah," she said. She smiled sadly. "Yes, of course it is."

"That will be seven dollars and forty-nine cents," the tech said as she pointed to the credit card machine. "Answer the questions on the screen."

"I'll pay cash."

Her tone was tight with annoyance. "You'll still have to answer the questions."

"Barb," Leila said. "Be nice to Nora. She's a good soul."

Barb shook her head then chuckled wryly. "If she's okay with you, Leila, then I guess she's okay with me."

I grinned. "Thanks for the vote of confidence." The screen had me confirm my identity and agree that I didn't plan to use the pills for any nefarious purposes. "They are serious about this."

"You'd be surprised at how many people find a reason to skedaddle when I ask them for their identification," Barb said, sliding the medicine box across the counter with the receipt.

I placed it in my purse. "Is the drug problem around here really that bad?" I had a flash of Fiona McKay snorting white powder off her hand.

Barb shrugged. "Most of the folks looking to buy are regulars, so it's hard to know for sure. You should ask the chief of police's wife." She nodded to Leila.

"Shawn doesn't bring work home with him," Leila said.

I knew that wasn't true. At least it hadn't been when we were married. He used to tell me all about his workdays over dinner. Maybe it was because I'd been the daughter of a cop. Or maybe because we hadn't had children. No little ears to hear all the nitty-gritty.

"Well, I better get back to the shop. It's so nice to see you again, Leila. Maybe we can get coffee sometime."

She smiled. "I'd really love that. How is Monday or Tuesday next week?"

I was startled at the invitation, but I rallied quickly. "Uhm, sure. Tuesday. One? At Moo-La-Lattes?"

"Perfect," Leila said. "It's a date."

On my way out the door, I remembered that I forgot to buy eye drops. As I made my way up the aisle with eye care products and vitamins, I overheard Leila say, "Thank you for arranging the donation drive. It could save a lot of lives."

"It's my pleasure, Leila. Anything for you and Shawn, you know that."

I hadn't heard of a donation drive going on in town. Were they raising money for charity? I made a mental note to offer Leila help when we met for coffee on Tuesday.

"Well, I'll be, Nora Black," said a cheery female voice. It was Fiona McKay, Reese's cousin. She had her thick hair in bouncy curls today, and she had a gorgeous glow about her skin. It was hard to reconcile this vibrant, healthy girl with the one I'd seen in her memory.

"Hi, Fiona. How are you doing today?"

"I'm good as hell." She grinned when she said it.

I recognized the title of Lizzo's hit song. It had become an anthem for Gilly after she'd broken things off with a guy, whose name I can't remember, but who'd ended up being another jealous jerk. She would play the song on full blast in a declaration of independence.

"I'm glad to hear it," I said. Fiona's smile was infectious. "You seem really happy this morning. Did you get good news?"

"You can say that," she said. She waved her left

hand, and I could see that she still wore the cuff bracelet, but a ruby and diamond ring adorned her left ring finger. She glanced over her shoulder then back to me. "I can't tell anyone yet."

"That's great."

Suddenly, Fiona tensed, her eyes darting away. She pivoted and stumbled, grabbing my purse arm to steady herself. "I'm so sorry, Nora," she said, all the joy gone from her face and her voice.

"It's all right," I said, trying to right myself.

Her gaze focused on someplace, or someone, behind me. "It was so nice to see you again. Reese told me you can be trusted."

It was a strange compliment. "Uhm...thanks. Are you okay?"

"Fine." She gave me a long look. "Goodbye, Nora."

"Uhm, bye." I hadn't even gotten the words out before she fast-walked down the aisle and around the corner.

I was so focused on Fiona's departure that I didn't notice the man who had just walked up behind me.

"Excuse me," the guy said. "Do I know you?"

I turned and nearly swallowed my tongue when I recognized him as Phil Williams, the manager of the Rose Palace Resort—Gilly's old boss, and the man responsible for a good portion of crime in Garden Cove.

Wait. Was he the one who'd scared off Fiona? Maybe. I mean, the guy scared the crap out of *me*.

I'd only seen Phil once, and that was when he'd fired

Gilly after her bogus arrest, and I'd had to drag her away before she could land herself another murder charge.

He was staring hard at me, and I realized I hadn't answered his question. An uncomfortable chuckle erupted, and then I said, "I don't believe so." I took my glasses from my purse and put them on to make a show of studying the eye drop bottles.

Phil didn't take the hint. "I know I've seen you."

"It's a small town," I said. My heart picked up a beat. This man was not above arson or murder for hire, and I didn't want to be on his radar. I shrugged, keeping my head down to read the ingredients on the Optic A bottle in my hand. "You can't help but cross paths with people sometimes."

A tall, balding man with glasses walked out of a side door. "Phil," he said, waving the local criminal boss toward him.

"Maybe I'll see you around," Phil said. He thrust his business card at me. "If you want to get a bite to eat sometime, give me a call."

When Hell froze over, I thought. I avoided eye contact as I took the card. After Phil disappeared into the backroom of the pharmacy, I put the bottle back on the shelf and practically raced out of the building. Much like Fiona had.

Holy crap. Phil Flippin' Williams, the man who'd fired my best friend from a job she loved, the man ultimately responsible for Carl Grigsby trying to kill me, and the man I most wanted to see behind bars, had just asked me out on a date.

CHAPTER 5

"*I* can't believe that scumbag hit on you!" Gilly balled her fists against her hips. "I'll kill him."

"For hitting on me?" I waved my hand at her. Six customers browsed in the shop, and all of them paused at my BFF's lethal proclamation. In a quiet voice, I added, "Maybe you shouldn't talk about killing someone in public. Remember what happened the last time."

Her drunk ex had shown up during our girls' get-together at the now-closed Bar-B-Q Pit and had attempted to intimidate me. Gilly had fiercely defended me, threatening to end Lloyd. The next day, she was charged with his murder.

Gilly whipped her gaze around the shop, and we both plastered on smiles.

"Just joking." She grabbed my elbow and took me aside, and in a much quieter voice, she said, "Are you going to tell Easy?"

I frowned at her. "I am. But not because the guy

flirted with me." Ezra had been investigating Phil Williams for a couple of months now, and as far as I knew, he hadn't been able to gather much evidence of the man's criminal activity. Phil had gone into a room with the pharmacy guy, which could have been for a myriad of legitimate reasons. "It's probably nothing, but he was meeting with a balding guy with glasses. I think it's the pharmacist."

Gilly nodded. "That would be Burt Adler. The description fits, anyhow."

"Oh, Burt Adler," Pippa said. She'd finished ringing up a customer and joined the conversation. "I heard his wife kicked him out of the house. He's been staying on his houseboat."

"It's good to know your time at the coffee shop is being spent wisely," I teased her.

"I actually heard this down the bread aisle at Walmart, thank you very much." She stuck her tongue out for punctuation. "I can always keep what I hear to myself," she shrugged, "you know, if you don't want to know any of the hot goss."

"No," Gilly said before I could. "You're like our very own Garden Cove Google."

I snickered. Then sneezed. "Ow." A pain blossomed in my lower back. I reached around to the aching spot. "Oh, damn." When I tried to move, it felt as if someone had grabbed my muscle just above my right buttock and was twisting the crap out of it. I hunched to the right, trying to get some relief.

"Are you okay?" Gilly asked. "What happened?"

"Flippin' sneeze," I wheezed on a whoosh of breath

as the pain increased. "I think I gave myself a back spasm."

"Do you need to go to the doctor?" Pippa asked. "We can close up shop and take you to the walk-in clinic."

"I don't think I can sit," I said. Bending at the waist intensified the constricting pain. "I need to lie down for a minute."

"Let's go to the massage room."

"Miss, how much for the rosemary and spearmint lotion?" a woman asked.

Pippa nodded to her. "I'll be right with you." Her brows wrinkled with concern. "I'll take care of the front. You let Gils work you over."

"I don't need a massage," I protested as another sharp twinge nearly dropped me to my knees.

Gilly ushered me into her section of the shop and led me into a quiet room. "I don't have a client for an hour. I'll see if I can loosen it up. You know the drill. You don't have to undress. Just climb on up and lie down with your face in the cradle."

I was not only Gilly's best friend, but I'd become one of her best customers. Since my hysterectomy, I hadn't recovered all my strength. Not ideal when I was dating a guy nearly two decades my junior. While I could keep up with Ezra in spirit, my body sometimes had other ideas. So, I got ninety-minute massages every couple of weeks, and the reflexology Gilly did on my arms, hands, and feet was like magic.

I felt like a slug as I crawled onto the padded table. Gilly flipped on the heat, and I immediately felt the warmth settle into my front side. She slipped off my low heels, slid a sheet over my body, and then placed heating pads over my low back. I took some deep breaths to relax. She turned up the sitar music.

"Do you want some aromatherapy?" she asked.

My nose had managed to get even stuffier in the face cradle. "Right now, someone could fart in a rosebush, and I wouldn't smell a thing," I said.

"You're such a poet." Gilly giggled. "Are you comfortable?"

"As I can be." I tried to slide my hip over a little more, but the smallest movement reengaged the spasm. "Distract me," I said. "How are the kids?"

She started rubbing my low back over the towels. "Marco can't stop singing his dad's praises. He's so impressed with Gio." I heard the sadness in her voice. "Ari is confused and angry. She won't talk to me about Vegas. I feel like she's hiding something, but she's at an age where I can't force her to tell me what's going on in her head."

I chuckled. "Ow." Note to self: no laughing during a back spasm. "Ari's always been headstrong." Ari was one of the most grounded and focused people I knew. I sometimes wished she would relax and not take everything so seriously, but the girl knew what she wanted—a highly prized scholarship to the California Institute of Technology—and she wouldn't let anything get in her way. "Do you want me to talk to her?"

"Would you?" Her finger pressure deepened. "She really trusts you."

"I can't promise I'll tell you what she says," I told

her. "That is, if she says anything at all. But if it's something you should know, I'll press her to confide in you."

"That's fair. I want Ari to be able to talk to someone she can trust when she's reluctant to turn to me. Someone who is smart and who loves her, so I'm okay if I don't get to know everything," Gilly said.

"You're a great mom," I told her.

In the next breath, she added, "But you will tell me if it's something bad and you can't convince her to tell me, right?"

I chuckled again. This time it hurt less. "If it's something really bad, then yes I will. You have my word. How are *you* doing?" I asked. "I can't believe Gio showed up without any warning."

"So typical," she said. "He came back to Garden Cove the same way he left, with no consideration for my feelings." She removed the heating pads and went to work with earnest on my muscles. "Why do I fall for jerks?"

"Because they aren't jerks when you fall for them," I said. "They only show their true selves after you've opened your heart to them."

"Well, this heart is closed. At least temporarily. After what happened with Lloyd, I don't trust my instincts when it comes to men." She started some percussion taps. "Hey, maybe now that you're dating Detective Hottie, you can prescreen any new men in my life."

"You want me to turn Ezra into your own personal dating app? Don't get me wrong, I would totally do it." Ezra did sort of owe me, but the request would definitely put a strain on our new relationship. However, for Gilly, I would risk the world.

"I'm kidding," she said, to my relief. "How are you feeling now?"

I wiggled my hips, and my back only twinged a little. "Better."

"Good. Now you won't have any excuse to back out of dinner tonight with Easy and Mason."

"Cripes. I forgot all about that." The wheels in my head started spinning. A back spasm was a perfectly valid excuse to get out of the obligation. I mean, it wasn't like I'd planned to get hurt. Allergies led to sneezing, and sneezing led to back pain. On the other hand, who threw their back out by sneezing? A fifty-one-year-old, out-of-shape woman, that's who. Did I really want to draw Ezra's attention to my fragility?

No. No, I did not.

SULLY'S SURF and Turf was situated between the Rose Palace Resort and Garden Cove Lake Condos out on Highway 44. It had a beautiful view of the lake from its deck seating, which was its main selling point. The seafood was frozen, not fresh, and even the catch-of-the-day specials were not local fish. However, they made tasty fried shrimp and hand-battered catfish.

When I'd gotten home that afternoon, I'd taken three ibuprofens and soaked in a hot bath for half an hour before dressing. I wore one of my tighter body shapers under jeans and a t-shirt to give my low back some support. I went through a dozen of my shoes until I found a pair of ankle-high boots that had no heel but were still fashionable. Unfortunately, my back still felt sore, but I was determined to not let it show.

Ezra had offered to pick me up. I'd told him I would meet him and Mason at Sully's, instead. If dinner with Ezra and Mason took an ugly or strange turn, I wanted to be able to make a quick escape.

I saw Ezra's big red truck in the parking lot and found a nearby spot to pull in. It was only seven o'clock, so the sun was still an hour out from setting, and since Sully's deck faced the west, it would give us a nice backdrop for dinner. At least we'd have some scenery to stare at if we ran out of conversation.

The place was packed, and a dozen people sat in the waiting area on wooden benches that lined the walls. I stood behind a family of seven in the entryway as the hostess took their name. She gave them a square plastic gadget and said, "When it lights up, your table will be ready."

The back of my throat still felt scratchy, but the Pseudo-Act seemed to be doing its job. I'd found some eye drops in my medicine cabinet, so at least I no longer looked like I might start bleeding tears at any minute.

"How many?" she asked.

"I'm meeting some people," I said. "I think they're here already."

"Name?"

"Holden," I said, leaned over to see if his name was on the list. "First name Ezra."

"Oh, you're with Easy." She raised her brows and gave me an appraising glance. I didn't care if I measured up. Her smile was amiable enough, but her gaze wasn't exactly friendly. "Follow me," she said. "They're out on the deck."

"Thanks, but I can find my way out there."

I headed through the dining room to the back of the restaurant. Was I making a mistake? Would this dinner be the beginning of the end for Ezra and me? I hoped not. Still, every part of me wanted to turn on my no-heel shoe and run far away.

When Ezra saw me through the glass window, his wide smile put a rod in my spine. I sucked up my fears and insecurities and crossed the distance to join him at a table next to the railing. A young man with hair past his ears and his head tilted down to look at his phone barely noticed my arrival.

Ezra stood up and, hot damn, he looked handsome. He wore jeans similar to the ones he'd had on the day before, and a collared, short-sleeved, dark blue button-down shirt. And, while I'd never been a fan of westerns, his tan suede boots conjured up all kinds of fantasies about riding a cowboy.

"Hi, Nora." He dipped down and kissed my cheek.

I tensed then forced myself to relax. "Hi back," I said, focusing my attention on Ezra. "Nice night."

"Sure is," he agreed. He pulled out the chair for me as he gestured to the teenager who didn't notice I was taking up space next to him. "This is Mason." He frowned. "Put your phone away, and say hello to Nora," he said to the kid.

Mason looked up and blinked, as if just noticing that there was a world going on around him. He nodded to me. "Hey."

"Hey," I said in return. I waited to see if he would say more.

He didn't.

Craptastic. It looked like the sunset was going to get a lot of play, because conversations would be in short supply.

"How was work today?" Ezra asked.

His warm gaze eased some of the tension still in my shoulders. "Busy. My allergies kicked up something awful, so Pippa made me work in the back so I wouldn't scare customers with my monster sneezes." I didn't mention the sneeze-initiated back spasm because I had my pride. "How have you been?"

"Good," he said. He reached across the table and squeezed my hand. He nodded toward the lake. "It's been pretty quiet so far, but I imagine with all the drunks on the lake, things will kick off soon."

We watched as two small yachts and three or four motorboats passed by. It was peaceful until a large pontoon drifted by with a group of young men who were in their early twenties, most of them shirtless. One held up a sign that read, "Show us your titties," as the rest of them held up beers, wiggled, shimmied, and shouted encouragement to the female diners. Humph. It was nice to see misogyny was alive and well in Garden Cove.

"It looks like the Memorial weekend kickoff has begun," I said.

Ezra laughed. "At least they spelled titties right. Last year, I saw at least two signs where guys spelled the same word with double Ds." He waggled his brows.

"Dad," Mason said, his tone embarrassed. "Gross."

I laughed.

Ezra glanced at Mason, whose gaze was glued to his phone. He was no different than Ari and Marco, who both treated their phones like extensions of their arms. They couldn't go five seconds without scrolling or tapping.

Ezra narrowed his gaze at the boatful of idiots. "It's just going to get worse from here. Rafferty has the uniforms working twelve-hour shifts this weekend to handle the drunks."

"Water patrol is going to have their hands full as well," I added.

My dad used to do the same thing on big summer holidays. It made sense for Shawn to follow suit. But I didn't say it out loud, because, while Ezra knew his boss was my ex-husband, I didn't want to constantly remind him.

He nodded. Then he pasted on a smile. "Mason's been helping me clean up the backyard at my place. We're going to look into getting a dog. Isn't that right, son?"

Mason shrugged. "Sure," he replied. *Tap. Tap. Tap. Scroll. Scroll. Scroll.* It didn't bother me. Marco used his phone to distract himself when he was stressed out. I imagined Mason used it in much the same way. And I imagined meeting me was the last thing on the kid's to-do list during his time with his dad. But I could tell that his seeming indifference bugged Ezra. I blew out a breath and made an effort to engage with the teenager. "Are you starting your senior year in the fall?"

"Yep," he said. To the phone.

"My best friend has twins in high school. Marco and Ari Rossi. You know either of them?"

He managed to pull his gaze away from the screen long enough to look at me. His eyes were green like his father's. "Yep."

"Uhm, are you looking at colleges?"

"Nope."

"Mason," Ezra said, his tone filled with warning. "You said you were interested in Blaston University. You said they had a good art program."

"Maybe." The boy shrugged.

"How about this weather?" I asked Ezra.

He frowned, then laughed. Then I laughed. Mason turned in his seat slightly to face away from us, which made me laugh again.

"This dinner is going so well," Ezra said.

"And we haven't even ordered food yet," I added.

Our waitress, a young brunette, came to the table. She plopped down menus in front of us. "I'm Tess. I'll be your server tonight. Can I get you folks something to drink?"

"I'll take Diet Coke," I said.

"I'll have an iced tea," Ezra ordered, "and Mason will have a—"

"Mountain Dew," the boy grunted out.

"Is Mellow Yellow okay?" Tess asked.

"Sure," he said, moving his gaze from his phone to

the menu. "Can we get spinach artichoke dip and chips and cheese sticks to start?" He glanced at his dad for approval.

Ezra gave a tiny shake of his head, but grinned. "Add bacon and cheese potato wedges." He looked at me. "Do you want any starters?"

"I think that's plenty of appetizers," I said.

"You'd think," said Ezra, grinning. "But you've never seen the Holden men chow down."

"I'm sure it's impressive." I looked at the waitress. "I'm good, thanks."

"Okay." Tess tapped her order pad. "I'll be back in a few minutes with your drinks and take your entrée orders."

"Perfect," said Ezra. "Thank you."

As soon as Tess left, I stood up from the table. My back was screaming at me to move and stretch. I didn't want to make a big show of it, but I needed to walk and work out the kinks I'd gotten from the ride over. "Please, excuse me," I told Ezra. "If Tess comes back for our orders. I'll take the blackened grouper with wild rice. Extra lemon aioli."

His brow furrowed. "Everything okay?"

"Fine," I said with a smile. "Just going to go wash my hands. If it's okay, I'll leave my purse here." I didn't want to haul it around with me. It weighed a couple of pounds with all the stuff crammed in there, and I didn't need my shoulder acting up in addition to my lower back. Getting old sucked.

"I'll keep your bag safe," said Ezra. "You sure you're all right?"

"Aces," I said, giving a thumbs-up. "Be right back."

Instead of heading to the bathroom, I walked through the restaurant and out the front door. A concrete sidewalk led to a path down to the lake. I wanted some privacy to do some yoga stretches, so I followed it around to the back. The restaurant sat on the edge of the lake, so the dock seating where I'd left Ezra and his son overhung the water by twenty or so feet. I stood right under it on a gravel bank that was only about four feet wide, where no one could see me.

I stretched from side to side, then did a standing forward bend. On my way up from the pose, I saw something red under the dock near one of the upright support posts, about halfway to the end of the structure.

I walked to the edge of the water for a closer look. A ripple in the water caused by a passing boat disturbed the red object enough that it rolled.

"Oh, no." I felt the blood drain from my face. Was that a person? "Hey," I shouted.

As ridiculous as it sounds, I waited for a second to see if the person would pop their head up. An arm floated to the surface. I recognized the cuff bracelet.

"No, no, no. Help! Someone help!" I shouted, hoping anyone from the restaurant might hear me as I kicked my boots off and waded out into the water. "Fiona!" I yelled, waist-deep in water, my feet sinking into the slimy muck as I made my way to her.

I've had to touch corpses before—my mother's, for one. It's unpleasant. Something happens to a body on a cellular level when life leaves it. Fiona's skin was a pale blue and as cold as the water surrounding us. I grabbed her, tugging her toward the bank. The action tweaked my back, but adrenaline and panic kept me going. "Help!" I cried out again. "Please, anyone!" My face was wet, and not just with splashing water. I wept for the girl who earlier in the day had acted so joyous, so full of life.

I stumbled back as the water grew shallow. Exhaustion overtook me as I sat on rock and mud. I pulled Fiona onto my lap. Her wide eyes were sightless, staring at nothing. I knew there was no point to starting CPR. She was gone. And she'd been gone for a while, given how cold and gray her skin looked.

"Nora!" I heard Ezra shout.

My arms and legs felt like lead. I didn't have the energy to crawl out from under the dock, so I shouted, "Down here. Under the dock. Please help!"

Within minutes, Ezra and a handful of other people were under the dock with me, hauling both Fiona and me to the shore.

I was soaked to the bone now, and with the sun setting, the chill made my teeth chatter.

Mason came up next to me. "A woman inside said an ambulance is on the way," he said breathlessly.

"I don't need an ambulance," I said. "And it's too late for Fiona."

Someone handed Mason a coat and the boy carefully wrapped it around me.

"Thanks, Mason," I said. Then I burst into tears. He awkwardly patted my shoulder as a crowd gathered closer to us and Ezra checked for Fiona's carotid pulse.

"Christ, Nora. What happened?" he said in a low voice.

"She was just there," I said as a pleasant numbness took over. I pointed out to the post. "She was just..."

"It's okay, Nora." He stood up, keeping himself between Fiona's body and the crowd of onlookers. He reached out and squeezed my shoulder. "It's okay."

I shook my head. "It's not. Fiona was here. Alive. Happy. And now she's gone. There's nothing okay about that."

CHAPTER 6

"She's Reese's cousin."

Ezra's expression tightened as he took in this information. "Okay. We'll get her notified."

As I studied Fiona's youthful, heart-shaped face, I found it difficult to reconcile the bubbly woman who'd preened about good news she couldn't reveal yet with the lifeless girl lying on the bank. She wore a red cocktail dress that was noticeably ripped, and her feet were bare. There was something else as well. She wasn't wearing the ruby and diamond ring she'd sported at the pharmacy. Had it slipped off in the water along with her shoes?

I was warmer now, and as the shock wore off, my fight-or-flight reflex was in complete flight mode. "I want to go home."

"Can you wait just a little bit? Maybe you and Mason can wait for the police in the parking lot," directed Ezra. "Give them a statement and let them know where to go."

"Of course." I could tell he wanted Mason away from the scene, and I felt like an idiot for not thinking of it myself. Getting the kid away from a dead body would have been Gilly's first move.

Ezra gave me a grateful nod. "Thanks, Nora."

Mason and I went out to the parking lot together. I was wet, mud up to my calves, and one glance in my car's sideview mirror told me I should have worn water-proof mascara. I looked like a drowned raccoon. Cripes. The thought made me sick. I was miserable, but at least I was alive. Poor Fiona.

"Did she fall off a boat?" Mason asked.

"Maybe," I said.

Mason rubbed his arms, his shoulders rounded, as he kicked a piece of gravel. He looked young. Lost. I was such an idiot. Seeing Fiona dead, even briefly, had shaken me. I could only imagine what it would have felt like when I was sixteen.

"Are you okay? Do you want to go home?" I asked Mason. "Or you can come home with me."

He shook his head. "I'll wait for my dad."

"I can stay with you if you don't want to be alone," I said.

He made a noise that could only be interpreted as disgust. He straightened his shoulders. "I'm good."

Great. I'm fairly certain I'd poked at his pride. "Well, I don't want to be alone."

"Yeah. You don't look so good." He leaned against my car. "How long do you think it will take Dad to finish up?"

"It could be a while." Drownings happened in

Garden Cove, more than the powers that be in this town would like for tourists to know. When my dad had been the chief of police, he'd had to deal with at least five drownings that I was aware of, and I was certain there had been more that he'd managed to keep under wraps. But it was a hazard of being a resort town situated on the water. And on a weekend like this, where the lake was packed with drunk tourists on boats, it was only by sheer luck that more people didn't fall overboard to their deaths.

Mason got on his phone and proceeded to ignore me. I rummaged through my purse and found my own. I created a group text with Gilly and Pippa.

I sent them a heart emoji because I wasn't sure what to write.

Three dots came up, then Gilly texted: *How's the date?*

Date over.

Pippa texted next. *The kid run you off with a pitchfork and torch?*

I'm not Frankenstein's monster, I sent back. Though I had died and been brought back to life, so the joke wasn't lost on me.

Then why is it over? Gilly asked.

Found someone in the lake. I couldn't bring myself to tell them that I'd personally found Fiona and had pulled her out of the water.

Three dots. Three dots. Three dots. Then nothing. My besties, for once, were at a loss for words.

Three dots again, then Gilly typed: *Tourist?*

Local. I answered. I wasn't sure if I should give them

Fiona's name. After all, her family hadn't been notified, yet. I decided to trust them to keep it to themselves. Pippa liked to gossip, but only with Gilly and me. *Keep it to yourselves until the family knows, but it's Fiona McKay.*

Gilly: *Wow. That's awful.*

Pippa: *Don't know who that is.*

She's Reese McKay's cousin. Just saw her yesterday. So heartbreaking.

I watched a balding man getting out of his car a few spaces down from me, and even without his white lab coat, I recognized him as Burt Adler, the pharmacist. I quickly typed, *can't talk call later*, and hit send.

I tucked my cellphone into my purse's side pocket as he walked past Mason and me. "I think they've closed," I told him.

Adler jerked to a startled halt. "Why?"

"They found a...uh, body in the lake." The words came easier if I didn't use Fiona's name.

"Do you know who?"

I shook my head.

Burt Adler took off toward the restaurant without so much as a thank you or goodbye. I saw him stop just outside the front door and talk to a man, shorter than him but the same slim build. They exchanged a few words before Adler trekked back to his car.

"I'm still hungry," Mason said.

I shook my head. Who could think about eating at a time like this? A growing boy, that's who. In a way, Mason reminded me of when I'd been a high school sophomore. I'd been gangly, awkward, and felt weird about my body. I wore a lot of oversized shirts to hide myself. Gilly had bloomed in eighth grade, but I hadn't even gotten my period until the end of the summer before our sophomore year.

"I'm sorry," I said. I wanted to distract the boy. Get his mind off the tragic evening. If that was even possible. "I bet your dad would pick you up something on the way home. Maybe from Taco Shake Shack."

"I love tacos," he said.

"Me too." Well, that was one thing we had in common. Mason was really slender, gangly. Ezra had told me that the boy ate more than he did. "You must have a hollow leg," I said.

"What's that mean?"

"You're in great shape is all. I wish I had your metabolism."

Mason shook his head. "I wish I could gain weight."

"Hey, you know. Give your body time. You're probably hungry because you're still growing. According to my friend Gilly, boys can keep growing until they're in their twenties. And once you stop growing up, I'm sure you'll start to fill out. I mean, look at your dad. He's pretty stacked."

Mason pulled a face.

"Sorry. I just mean, he's not super skinny. I'm sure you got some of his genes."

"Mom says I look a lot like dad did when he was my age."

I blinked at Mason. He was sixteen, the same age Ezra had been when he'd gotten Kati pregnant and married her. I couldn't even imagine what kind of stress that must have been for him. Now that I really looked at Mason, I could see Ezra in the deep set of his eyes, the high cheekbones, and his wide mouth.

I smiled at Mason. "Then your dad was pretty cute when he was your age," I said.

Mason stared at me, and as serious as can be, he said, "Aren't I a little young for you?"

I felt like I'd been punched in the throat. "I didn't mean it like that. I only meant to say, that your mom is right, you do look like your dad."

Mason laughed hard enough that he was snorting on every third or fourth guffaw.

"Got ya," he said, still laughing.

"Ha ha," I said flatly. "Not funny."

"I'm sorry, Nora," he chuckled. "But your face. Priceless."

I chuckled. "Yeah, yeah, you got me."

He nodded. "Hey, I was just joking. So, don't tell my dad. He ordered me to be nice to you."

"Ordered you, huh?" Still, I felt like I should address the fifty-one-year-old cougar in the parking lot. "Does it bother you that we're going out?"

"Why would I care?"

Oh, lawd, he was going to make me say it. "Because of my age."

Mason frowned. "What about it?"

"Because I'm older than your dad."

"You're both old," he said with the casualness of youth. "Besides, there's the same age difference between Mom and Roger."

Okay, so I was starting to love this kid. "You're wise beyond your years."

He smirked. "I've been told that by my mom, too."

"Nora!" I looked toward the embankment as Ezra waved and trotted across the lot to us.

He gave Mason a quick, reassuring shoulder squeeze, then asked me, "Can we talk for a moment?" He nodded toward his truck.

"Sure," I said.

"Mason, stay here. I need to ask Nora a few questions. We'll be right back."

Mason shrugged, but the grooves deepened between his furrowed brows. "Whatever," he said.

I followed Ezra to the other side of his truck. "Did you get ahold of Reese?" I asked.

"Chief told me he'd make the death notification."

"Good," I said.

"How do you know Fiona McKay?" he asked.

I frowned. "I ran into Fiona yesterday outside the courthouse, then again this morning at the pharmacy."

"What was your sense of her?"

"Do you mean intuition or sense? As in my gut feeling, or my scratch-n-sniff visions?"

"Either," he said. "Both, actually."

"I liked her. She seemed...sweet." I didn't want to speak ill of the dead, but I couldn't hide the vision I'd gotten about Fiona. "The first time I met her, I got a scent vision. I saw a memory of a man giving her drugs."

"Do you know who?"

"Unless his real name is Sugar, I have no idea."

"Seriously?" Ezra asked.

"Yep."

He tilted his head at me. "Was it a boyfriend?"

"Maybe. They were definitely friendly. He had red and black pointy-toed cowboy boots on, if that helps any."

Ezra cringed. "Fancy."

"That's what I thought."

He took my hand. "Sorry about tonight."

"Me, too." I swallowed the knot in my throat. "I just saw Fiona today, Ezra. She seemed...jubilant. I..." I shook my head. "What do you think happened? It looks like she was dressed up for a party. Maybe she'd been on one of those yachts. She had a ring on earlier today, but it isn't on her finger now." What if whoever had given her the ring took it back? She could have done some binge drinking to forget. Only, I hadn't smelled any alcohol on her when I'd pulled her from the water. "Do you think she had too much to drink and just..." I made a dive motion with my hand.

"I didn't see any obvious evidence of foul play," Ezra said. "But the coroner and the medical examiner will have the final say." He snuck a quick kiss. "I miss you."

Those three little words quickened my pulse. "Do you have to stay here?"

"It's probably an accidental drowning, and the water patrol is stopping all the boats to see if anyone saw anything. There's nothing really left for me to do here tonight."

I cupped his cheek. "You look exhausted," I told him. Or maybe I was projecting. I was sad, tired, wet, and sore. The combination had me yearning for my bed. "You and Mason should head home. I think he's rattled."

"I'm sorry our date took a terrible turn."

"I'm sorry, too. For a lot of reasons. That poor girl."

He pressed his forehead to mine. "I'll call you tomorrow."

"I'd like that."

* * *

BY THE TIME I got to work the next day, my back ached as if someone had taken a jackhammer to my spine. It certainly wasn't emergency-room worthy, but if it kept up, I would call my doctor. I probably just needed a good muscle relaxer and a few days of rest. Unfortunately, since it was Friday, and Memorial weekend was in full swing, neither of those things were going to happen.

Pippa and Gilly had tried to talk me into staying home, but I knew if I'd stayed home, I would've had finding Fiona on a constant loop in my head. I still thought about her today, but the shop and its customers gave me enough distractions to keep me from letting her death overwhelm me.

However, allergies didn't care about your emotional or physical well-being, so by the afternoon, my throat was scratchy and my sneezes epic. I'd taken the Pseudo-Act, Claritin, and the nasal spray, and the combination of meds made my skin feel buzzy.

"You're glassy-eyed," Pippa said. "Are you sure you don't want to go home?"

I pshawed at her with a quick wave. "If I took days off for allergies, you wouldn't see me until September." Truthfully, I had cried on the way to work. Fiona had been so young, still in the bloom of her life, and now she was gone. It was tragic, and it had stirred up emotions in me about my mother. Most days I could think about Mom without falling apart, but today was not most days.

Gilly's last client had been at noon, so she'd gone home for the day. While the morning had been busy, the afternoon had slowed down considerably. There was only one guy in the shop right now, a tall man with short dark hair and graying sideburns who was studying the ingredients on the men's shampoo bottle. This was the fifth time this month he'd been in the store, but the first time he actually looked interested in buying something.

"There are no parabens, waxes, or sulfides in our shampoos," I told him.

He shrugged. "I'm allergic to apple pectin. It makes my head itch, so I always check the label."

With my allergies, I knew all about itchy. I gave him a bright smile. "Well, it's your lucky day. There is no apple pectin in any of our products."

While the man shopped, I went into the workroom to grab a box of soaps to restock a nearly half-empty shelf.

When I came back out, I sneezed, and yipped at the quick stab of pain in my low back.

Pippa crossed her arms and glared at me. "You should go. I've got this."

"I'm right as rain," I told her. "I have no plans to leave you on your own with the holiday crowd."

"There's one guy in here." He looked up at her. She

gave him a polite smile. "And we're glad you're here." In a harsh whisper to me, she said, "Fine, if you insist on staying, I insist on some intel. I know your date went south last night, and you don't want to talk about Fiona," Pippa said. "But I have to know. How was it with Easy's son up until then?"

"Fine. Kids love me." I opened the box of soaps and started shelving them. "Did we sell all the chocolate-mint soap yesterday?" The chocolate-mint was part of a new ice cream scents line I was trying out. I'd designed them to look like scoops of mint chocolate-chip ice cream and had packaged them in plastic parfait cups. We'd had twenty on the shelf yesterday.

"Okay, Miss Avoidance," she said. "Hint taken. And, yes, a lovely woman all the way from Chicago bought what we had. She said they were adorable and would make wonderful gifts."

"That's fantastic." I'd needed a pick-me-up, and hearing that someone loved the soaps enough to want to share them made me happy. "My next batch should be completely cured by tomorrow. I'm thinking about making a Neapolitan soap, chocolate, vanilla, and strawberry, and sliced to look the way my mom used to cut the ice cream on special occasions."

"Yum," Pippa said. "We could do a rum raisin, too."

I scrunched my nose. "Nobody likes rum raisin."

"I do."

"Weirdo."

She laughed. "It's really good."

"Yuck." And success. We were no longer talking about me and my disaster of a date.

Pippa went to the cash register to ring up the customer who had decided on an argan oil shampoo with tea tree and peppermint, great for dandruff, and a coconut conditioner that was surprisingly popular with men. The secret was using coconut cream from the milk, and not coconut oil. It was nourishing to the hair, and bonus, it smelled like a day in the tropics.

More customers came into the shop, and soon, Pippa and I were too busy to chat, which suited me fine. And for a short while, I was able to forget about Fiona McKay and her heartbreaking demise. For a short while...

"I heard she was a waitress out at Portman's on the Lake," a short woman with khaki shorts and a red tank top said.

Her friend, taller but rounder, wore a pale-yellow sundress and sandals. She nodded. "I heard she killed herself over a married man."

"Really? I was told it was an accident. From what I hear, she had a history of drinking. A real party girl, if you get my drift."

The entire shop got her drift. I clenched my fists.

The sundress lady said, "Either way. If you live hard, you can't blame anyone if you die young."

My ears burned at the insinuation that Fiona had somehow deserved her fate because of her reputation. I slapped my hand down on a display case harder than I'd intended, but it got their attention. I faked cheerful civility. "Can I help you all find anything today?" I asked with a tight smile.

"Just browsing," Khaki Shorts said.

"We heard your shop had some great creams. We live a town over," Yellow Sundress added, even though I hadn't asked. I could give two craps where they came from, considering it was taking everything inside me to not tell them where they could go. "We like to shop local when we can."

"Hell nice. How, I mean. How nice. Well, you just let me know if you need any assistance." I'd be happy to help them pull their heads out of their asses.

Pippa took my elbow and guided me away from them. "Those two bitches are not worth it," she told me, reminding me why I loved her so much. "I'll upsell the crap out of them, and we'll take our revenge by taking their money."

"Have I told you lately how awesome you are?"

Pippa snorted. "Not nearly as often as you should."

"Well, then let me just say it again. You're awesome."

The door chimed and my knees wobbled as Reese McKay, her hair pulled back in a tight bun and she was wearing her uniform, hurried toward me. "Can I talk to you?"

"Sure," I said. "Uhm, in private?"

"Yes. Can we step outside?"

"Let's go back into the massage room, it's quiet and soundproof." I wasn't sure what she was going to say to me, but just in case it included yelling and crying, it seemed like the safest place to take her.

Reese nodded then gestured for me to lead the way. Once inside the room, Reese closed the door behind her. Her energy was manic, and frankly, it made me nervous.

"I'm so sorry about your cousin," I said. "Such a dreadful accident." I couldn't get Fiona's visage out of my mind. I rubbed my fingers together as I remember how cold her skin felt.

The young cop banged her hand against the door. "This wasn't an accident. You were there, Nora. You found her. You had to have seen something—anything —that might help me discover what happened to her."

"She drowned," I said. Her sudden outburst shook me. "I know it can be hard to accept."

"No," Reese said. The anger in her voice was replaced with anguish. "This was not an accident, Nora. Fiona didn't just fall off a boat and drown. I won't believe it."

"Is this your gut?" I asked, trying to be supportive. I understood the need to lash out, to try and find something or someone to blame when it came to loss. I got stupid irate with my mom's doctor when he'd told us that her cancer had progressed to a point where treatment might give her a few extra months, but only if we were lucky. "Or did the medical examiner find any evidence that her death might be something more...sinister?"

"They're leaning toward an accident for now, but—" She shook her head. "Fiona was an excellent swimmer, and her blood alcohol was only point-zero-one. I've seen that girl swim a pond twice around on a fifth of whiskey."

"What about drugs?"

Her mouth opened, and she looked as if she might punch me.

"I saw something in a vision," I clarified.

Reese sighed then nodded. "Outside the courthouse."

"Yes."

"I wondered." She sighed again. "Even so, I know there's something more going on with her death, and I owe it to my aunt and uncle to find out." She took her phone from her pocket and opened her voicemail. "She sent this to me yesterday, and she mentioned you." Reese pushed play on a message that had Fiona's name and was dated for four forty-two yesterday afternoon, only a couple hours or so before she was found.

Reese, please call me as soon as you can. Fiona's voice was shaky. Emotional. *I've screwed up bad. I know you said not to call you, but this time...I...I'm in real trouble. I promise, this is the last time. Please call. If... If something happens to me, tell Nora Black thanks for the hand."*

"I ignored her. I ignored the call. She's dead, and it's my fault." Reese gripped my hand. Tears crowded her eyes. "She knew something bad was coming. So, please, please, Nora. Help me."

CHAPTER 7

*M*y chest pinched with anxiety. Fiona had sounded distraught, and the message had come shortly before she'd been found in the lake. Coincidence? Maybe. But I understood why Reese wanted to believe it was foul play. Guilt was a powerful motivator. "Have you played Fiona's message for Ezra?"

"Yes, but he said it's not evidence of wrong-doing. Not even circumstantially. Fiona doesn't say how she's in trouble or with who." She put her phone away. "I even went to the chief. The voicemail isn't enough to open up an official investigation."

"I get it," I said. I knew my words might fall on deaf ears. I said them anyways. "You can't blame yourself for what happened to your cousin. There's nothing to say that answering her call would have changed the outcome."

"I don't need a therapy session, Nora. I need practical help."

I shook my head. "I'm not a detective." My stomach

felt sour. "Coming to me is the most impractical thing you can do."

Reese McKay circled her pert nose with a finger. "You can tap into that supernatural sense of smell of yours and find out what really happened to my cousin. Fiona had her problems, but she didn't deserve to die."

Empathy welled within me. I wanted to help Reese. Still. My gift wasn't exactly reliable. And I wasn't sure Reese was right about Fiona being murdered. "I can't predict how or when I'm going to have a vision, and I certainly can't pick and choose what memories I see. It doesn't work that way."

"You solved two murders, one of which was a cold case from ten years ago, Nora. If anyone can help me, it's you." She reached out and took my hand. "I know I can't bring her back. But I can get her justice. I knew Fiona better than anyone...she was like a little sister to me. I'm telling you, she was murdered."

I admired her staunch belief in her cousin. I'd felt the same way when Gilly was accused of killing her ex, even with all the evidence stacked against her. Reese's request for me to use my aroma-mojo to look into Fiona's death made my inner alarm bells ring. Yet, all my excuses seemed lame in comparison to her heartache. "I can't promise you anything, Reese," I said, lightly squeezing her hand and letting it go. "But I'll try."

Her visible relief made my stomach roil. Reese was putting a lot of faith into my sniffer's ability. More than I had.

I recalled how distracted Fiona had looked in the pharmacy when Phil Williams had shown up. It certainly hadn't taken her long to make herself scarce. Could he have been part her of her *trouble?* "Did Fiona know Phil Williams?"

"Not that I know of." She peered at me, her eyes crinkling at the corners. "I mean, of course, she knew *of* him. He's a major player in the resort business in town. But she'd never mentioned him to me. Why?"

"When I saw her at the pharmacy yesterday, she'd seemed nervous right before Phil Williams walked down the aisle where we were standing."

Fiona shook her head. "I wish I knew more about Fiona's life, but she wasn't forthcoming with her personal life. Mostly because she knew I wouldn't approve. Damn it. I hope she wasn't involved with Williams. He's the worst kind of scum." She rubbed her palms against her pants "I think your best bet is to start with Players Restaurant at Portman's on the Lake," Reese said. "Fiona told my aunt Jenny that she was working last night, and as far as I know, it's the only job Fiona has...*had*."

Well, crap. Gio was the new head chef of Players Restaurant. The last thing I wanted to do was get anywhere near him. I'm sure the place would be packed with tourists, so hopefully, he'd be too busy to leave the kitchen. He'd only been in town for two days and wouldn't know anything about the girl, so I didn't need to talk to him.

I thought about the missing ring. "What about her boyfriend? Would he know what she was up to?"

"Fiona didn't have a boyfriend." Reese hunched her shoulders. "That I know of. Damn it, Nora. I've been keeping my distance from Fiona for the past couple of months. The DUI had kind of been the last straw for me. She told me she was getting her shit together, but..." Reese held her hands out, palms up. "I didn't want to hear it. And now she's gone."

"Okay," I said. "I'll do my best for you. But Reese, you have to be prepared for answers you might not like."

"I know," she said, tears gathering in her eyes. "I know."

AT THE END of the workday, my cellphone rang. It was my generic ringtone, which meant it was most likely a spam call, but I checked it anyway. It came up on my display as Garden Cove Police Department. Was it Ezra? No. He would have called me on his cellphone.

On the next ring, I picked up the call. "This is Nora Black," I said.

"I'm aware," said a familiar voice. "I called you, after all."

"Hello, Shawn." Why in the world was my ex-husband calling me? We hadn't talked since the Lloyd Briscoll case. While we'd left things cordial, with Shawn thanking me for my help, he'd given me the impression that he hoped to never cross paths with me in a professional setting again. I think my new ability freaked him out, especially since it had given me vulnerable glimpses of his home life. "What can I do for you?"

"I...uhm, Leila. She said she ran into you in town

yesterday. You all are having lunch or something next week."

"Yep," I confirmed with a tiny bit of trepidation. "On Tuesday. That's okay with you, isn't it? I just, well, I like Leila."

"I'm not trying to keep you away from her," he said. I detected a hint of defense in his tone. "That's not the reason I'm calling."

"Oh. Good. So...why are you calling?"

He paused, then said, "I'm worried about her. I wondered if maybe you might have...you know," he made sniffing noises, "seen something."

Oh, lord. I was beginning to feel like the local crystal ball. "My sinuses were clogged when I ran into Leila, and since my gift is tied to my ability to smell, it would have been impossible to get any kind of reading." I was glad I didn't have to lie, because if I had seen something Leila wanted to keep private, I'm not sure I would have told Shawn.

"She's been acting different lately," he said.

"How so?"

"Like she's...I don't know. Not herself."

I didn't know Leila well, so I wasn't sure what "acting different" entailed, but she had seemed fine to me when I'd run into her. Good, even. But Shawn sounded worried. "She mentioned getting off chemo a month ago. Maybe she's still dealing with side effects."

"Maybe. She was supposed to start a new round last week, but her doctor says her immune system isn't bouncing back from the last three-month course. She can't take it again. Not until her white blood cell counts are back up." His voice choked.

"I'm sorry, Shawn. I didn't know."

"She's putting on a brave face," he said. "If the cancer doesn't turn around in the next week or two, the doctor says a bone marrow transplant might be our best option." He paused again. "The boys are getting tested, just in case. And the hospital is doing a donor drive to test as many folks as possible."

That must have been what Barb the pharmacy tech had been talking to Leila about when she'd said donation drive. Tears burned my eyes and my nose started dripping again. Talk of chemo, failing immune systems, and treatments took me back to last year, when I had watched my mother fight for her own life. The cancer had won the war.

I hated to think of Leila winning so many battles, like Mom, only for none of it to matter in the end. "There's hope," I said to him. "I'm sure a donor match will be found. That's something to hold on to."

"You're right," he conceded.

In the background, a man said, "Here you go, Chief. That medical report you asked for."

"I better let you go," Shawn said. "Thanks, Nora. I'm sorry I bothered you with this."

I felt a rush of empathy for Shawn. "It's okay. I do care about you, and I like Leila a lot. I'll keep you both in my thoughts."

"I appreciate it."

"One thing," I said quickly before he could hang up.

"I guess you heard I was the one to find Fiona McKay last night."

"I heard. I'm sorry. I know it must have rattled you. I shouldn't have called with my problems. I didn't think... Are you okay?"

"Yes." As far as I knew, Shawn wasn't aware that Ezra and I were dating. I wouldn't lie about it if he asked me directly, but I would avoid the subject if I could. It was a long shot that he'd tell me anything, but I had to try. "Do you think it was an accident?"

"I do," he said, surprisingly forthcoming. "Fiona McKay was a troubled girl."

"Has anyone figured out where she went into the water?"

He paused. "Not yet. Water patrol is searching up and down the lake today."

"So, no evidence that it might not have been an accidental drowning?"

"Did you get some kind voodoo vision that showed you something different?"

"No," I admitted. "It's...well, she was just so young. I'm curious is all. I met the girl recently and she made an impression."

"Don't go digging around," Shawn said. "You'll just stir up things that are better left alone. Her family doesn't need to know about all the stuff she got up to. They should be allowed to grieve for her without all that disillusionment."

"Because of the drugs?" I asked.

"How did you know about the drugs?"

Great. I'd overplayed my hand. "I did get a vision

when I first met her. Nothing about her death, but I witnessed an unsavory moment in her personal life that involved drugs."

Shawn sighed. "I'm going to tell you something, but I'm going to trust you to keep it between us. You can't even tell Gilly."

"Whatever you tell me will stay between us," I swore. I hated keeping anything from my best friend, but since Fiona McKay had nothing to do with Gilly, I didn't see it being an issue.

"I'm looking at the medical examiner's report, and Fiona had opioids in her system. Not enough to kill her, but enough to slow her reaction time. There was water in her lungs, no wounds on her body, except for some bruises on her upper arms that looked to be a week old and some fresh ones on her shins that could have been from anything, including an accidental fall off a boat. Other than that, no signs of a struggle, and the medical examiner and the coroner have ruled it was accidental. Normally, I wouldn't care if you wanted to waste your time looking into a drowning, but Fiona McKay has other secrets that shouldn't come to light, for her family's sake."

"Like what?"

He hesitated, then said, "I'm trusting you."

"I understand."

"Frank Lopez, a vice detective in Rasfield, arrested Fiona for methamphetamines three months ago." Rasfield was a small lake town in the next county over, but only about fifteen miles from Garden Cove. It was a popular destination for people who liked to camp. "She had enough on her for a felony charge of possession with intent to distribute."

"She was selling meth?" I inhaled a sharp breath. "Does Reese know?" Fiona had come from an affluent family with lots of money. Why would a girl like that turn to drug dealing?

"No," Shawn said. "And I don't want her to find out. Fiona gave up intel on her distributor that led to an arrest. Lopez was able to flip him for an even bigger deal. In exchange, he expunged Fiona's arrest and kept her part of the investigation off the record. Her family didn't know when she was alive, and there's no reason for them to know now that she's dead."

"Aren't you worried that her death might be a result of someone finding out she was a snitch?"

"I called Lopez this morning. He says he retired her file after the arrests, especially since she wouldn't have to testify. She shouldn't have been vulnerable to any breach."

"Do you think Fiona kept up her...side job?"

"Christ, Nora. No. She's had to check in with Frank every month. He even made her do mandatory drug screens. According to him, she's been clean since her arrest. He did say that she missed her appointment last week, though. It was the first time. Damn it. I've watched Fiona grow up in this town. For a while, I really thought she was pulling her life together." I could imagine him scrubbing his face in frustration the way he used to do when he was aggravated with me. "Now, leave this one alone, okay," he said stiffly. "The medical examiner says

Fiona McKay's death was accidental. Let her rest in peace."

I believed Shawn's motives. His protective nature was one of the things that had drawn me to him when I was fifteen. Being the chief of police's daughter had its downsides, like the way kids used to call me a narc. Having Shawn in my corner had gotten me through the worst of it. But when we were married, his shielding nature had stifled me. He'd sometimes made decisions for us—for me—in an effort to "protect" me.

This phone call was evidence that not much had changed in Shawn when it came to the people he loved. Instead of talking to Leila and asking her why she'd been acting different, he'd gone behind her back to me to avoid adding to her distress. Now, he was doing the same thing to the McKays—protecting them from truths about their own daughter.

"Most people aren't fragile dolls, crumbling at the first sign of pressure." Maybe if Reese knew about Fiona's past, it would give her some closure. Or maybe it would make her even more determined that Fiona had been murdered. "The truth is the truth, Shawn. Avoiding it doesn't help anyone. Fiona's family should know what was going on in her life. Let them grieve and accept everything so they can move forward."

"I'm doing what's best for everyone," said Shawn, his tone final. "If you get one of your...er, visions that show she was murdered, call me. I'll make sure we investigate. Right now, I don't want to cause her parents any unnecessary pain. Promise me you'll keep what I've told you to yourself."

I didn't want to make that promise because I didn't feel right about withholding information from Reese. I worried that Shawn's overprotective nature would lead to more grief for Fiona's family.

"Nora?"

"I heard you," I said. "I understand."

"Good," said Shawn. We said our goodbyes and ended the call.

In the corporate world, I'd learned a lot about the gray language of contracts. I'd told Shawn what he needed to hear, but I did not promise him anything.

In the end, I would follow my own conscience if it meant getting closure or justice for Fiona.

CHAPTER 8

The next day, I went to Gilly's house to have a chat with Ari. My BFF wanted my visit to look like a happy accident, not a planned intervention, but when I arrived, Ari wasn't home.

"She's at a friend's house. Jonathan Driver. His mom, Robbin, cuts hair at the Garden Cove Style," said Gilly as she let me into the house. We crossed the living room and went into the kitchen. I sat down on a stool at the breakfast counter. "Ari should be back soon."

There were several stylists who worked out of the shop. A young woman named Toni cut my hair every six weeks, but I didn't know the other beauticians' names. "Is she the one with the blonde A-line bob?" I asked.

"No, that's Jennifer. Robbin is the one with the two-tone purple-pink hair."

"Oh, sure. She's always really nice. So, is this Jonathan a romantic interest?"

"You tell me," Gilly scoffed. "The day Ari talks

about her romantic life with me is the day snakes grow legs and go for a run."

I laughed. "Why not wings?"

"What do you mean?"

"Why give the snakes legs to run and not wings to fly?"

She gave me an *are you stupid?* look. "Because the idea of flying snakes is terrifying."

"This is true," I said, smiling as I put my elbows on the counter. I looked at the space that used to hold Gio's prized knives. After one of them, a filet knife, had been used to kill her abusive ex-boyfriend, Gilly had donated the set to an auction to support the local women's shelter. They'd been worth almost three grand, and I was glad to see them sold for a worthy cause.

Gilly poured us both some iced tea then joined me. "How are you?" she asked as she set the tall glass in front of me. "It must have been awful finding that poor girl."

"It was beyond awful," I said. "I'm not squeamish. I've seen death before, but never in one so young or healthy. That's the part that's difficult to come to terms with."

"I don't know what you were thinking, Nora, jumping in the water like that."

"I had to get her. I couldn't leave her out there. You know?" I debated for a half a second about keeping my covert investigation into Fiona's life from Gilly. "I'm going to Players tonight," I said.

She stiffened. "To spy on Gio?"

"Uh, no. I have no interest in what that ass is doing as long as it doesn't involve you."

"Then why?" Gilly stretched her neck side to side. "He hasn't called me or the kids since the other night. I'm just waiting for the really big shoe to drop."

"My reasons have nothing to do with him, but you know that if I get any vibe about Gio, I won't hesitate to clue you in."

"I know. So, tell me why we're going to eat at Players tonight."

I cracked a smile. "I didn't say we."

"I'm pretty sure the *we* was implied." She crooked her head at me. "How are we going to manage to get in? Portman's on the Lake has flyers all over town about their brand-new, award-winning chef." Her face soured as if the accolades tasted bitter in her mouth, but she quickly shrugged it off. "I can't imagine they'll have any openings for a while."

"I didn't see any flyers." The resorts usually dropped off flyers to local businesses when they had a special event.

"I threw it away when Lucinda brought it by this morning. You were in the back. I drew dicks all over Gio's name first and was going to tape it up outside, but Natalie, the spa manager at Portman's, sends me her overflow when she's heavily booked."

I chuckled and gave her a wry smile. "I still would have put it up. We have a seven forty-five dinner reservation, by the way."

She tucked her chin. "That's amazing."

"I'm that good." I grinned. "At least my products

are. Twyla Reynolds is the hostess for Players. I recognized her name when I called to see if there were any reservations available. She loves my face products. I promised her a jar of her favorite wrinkle cream in exchange for squeezing me in." I'd dropped a jar into my purse before I'd left work to give her as a thank-you.

"You still haven't told me why you want to eat there. It has to be a good reason if you're giving away sixty dollars' worth of product."

"Because of Fiona McKay. She worked there as a waitress."

"All right," Gilly said with some caution. "And why is that important?"

"Reese dropped by the shop this afternoon after you left for the day. She wants me to look into Fiona's death."

Gilly's frown deepened. "What? Isn't that what the police are for?"

I tapped the side of my nose. "They don't have my scent powers. Besides, Reese doesn't believe her cousin died accidentally."

"You can't predict when or what you see with that super-sniffer of yours."

"I told her that. She still wants me to try." I shook my head. "Fiona called her a few hours before she was found drowned. Reese screened the call and let it go to voicemail."

Gilly let out a noisy breath. "Wow."

"Exactly. She's devastated with guilt."

"I can imagine."

"And, if that isn't awful enough, Fiona mentioned me in the message."

"Really? I thought you had just met her."

"Exactly. So, I have no idea why she told Reese I'd given her a hand. Frankly, I'm at a loss. I tried to talk her out of digging deeper. Fiona's death is most likely an accident, and I'm afraid any memories I see will open wounds that have nothing to do with her drowning."

"Like what?"

Like her stint as a drug dealer, I thought. "Drugs. Maybe worse."

"What did Detective Hot Stuff have to say about you starting your own psychic detective business?"

"I'm not starting anything of the sort." I picked at a stray hair sticking to my shoulder. "And I haven't told Ezra. Yet."

"Nora." She said my name as if it were an admonishment. "You should tell him. Besides, he could help. After all, he's got a direct line to the evidence."

I wrinkled my nose at her. "I'll tell him."

"Good. Nothing ruins a relationship like secrets."

Unhappily, secrets seemed to be the soup of the day.

I couldn't stop thinking about Fiona's biggest secret. How in the world had a girl like Fiona McKay, from a good family, ended up selling drugs?

The instant the thought entered my head, I knew it was silly. There were plenty of law breakers who came from good homes and just as many upstanding folks who had crappy childhoods. But with a cop for a cousin, and parents who leased most of the commercial real estate in town, how did she think she could get away with illegal activities without anyone finding out? Maybe she'd wanted to get caught. Some kind of cry for help. She wouldn't be the first person to act out self-destructive behavior in order to get her family's attention.

I wondered if anyone at Portman's or Players knew about Fiona's old side business. Reese had said her cousin had been a waitress there for two years. It seemed like she would have bonded with one or two co-workers.

I sighed. I hated to think about drugs infiltrating our little resort town. I'd lived in urban areas where stuff like drug trafficking was always on the news, but I guess I'd never considered Garden Cove a hotbed of vice. But since I'd returned, I'd discovered blackmail, arson, murder, and now drug dealers. Unfortunately, now that I knew it existed, it was hard not to let it color my view of the town.

Every time I thought about organized crime in this area, I just assumed it had to do with Phil Williams. But maybe he was just one of many bad seeds in Garden Cove. Carl Grigsby, the dirty cop who'd tried to kill me, had confessed to me that Phil Williams had been behind the fires that consumed two of our town's most beloved restaurants, including my favorite barbeque place. He'd gotten Grigsby on the hook with blackmail. But that didn't make the guy a criminal kingpin, did it?

I knew one thing for certain, I'd sleep a lot easier when Ezra found enough evidence to put Phil away. If the guy had anything to do with Fiona's death, accidental or otherwise, I would find a way to have him crucified. But really, the quickest solution to the Williams problem would be for Carl Grigsby to wake up from his coma and testify against the Godfather of Garden Cove.

Wouldn't that be a nice win for the good guys?

"A dollar for your thoughts," Gilly said.

"I do love a good cost-of-living increase," I told her. "But I'm not sure my thoughts are worth a whole dollar."

She smiled. "I don't like seeing you troubled like this, Nora. I know it's for a reason, but still. You've been through a lot, and you deserve a break."

"Unfortunately, life doesn't come with a pause button." Her hand was on the counter, and I cupped it with mine. "We're okay," I told her. "The two of us. Life has dealt us both crappy and awesome hands, and we not only survive, we thrive."

Gilly laughed. "I'm getting that put on a t-shirt."

"I'd prefer a t-shirt that says, *I love tacos*."

She shrugged. "Same thing."

I took a sip of my tea. Sweet and no hint of bitterness. Just like Gilly. "So, you're coming with me tonight, then?" I was actually relieved. I had no idea if I would uncover anything at the restaurant, so I hadn't wanted to go to dinner alone. Having Gilly for backup in case things got super creepy was a good idea.

"Yes. I wouldn't miss it." There was a distant bang sound. Gilly unexpectedly stood up. "Did you hear that?

"Car door, maybe."

"It's probably Ari," she said in a hushed voice.

"Okay."

"Act natural."

I smirked. "Take your own advice, girl."

She smacked my arm.

"Ow."

"Oh, I didn't hurt you," Gilly said dismissively. We heard the front door open. A few seconds later, Ari walked into the kitchen.

The teenager's short hair was slicked back on the sides and the top styled into a '50s quiff. She wore cut-off jeans, a white t-shirt with rolled-up sleeves, and a pair of light blue Converse low tops.

She barely glanced at us as she walked over to the fridge, opened the door, and grabbed a juice. She popped the top and took a sip. Gilly and I watched her as if she were a rare species of animal on *Wild Kingdom*.

Ari stopped mid-sip and looked at us. "You guys are being extra."

"Extra cool?" Gilly asked.

"Extra beautiful?" I added helpfully.

Gilly kept it going. "Extra smart."

"Extra charming."

"Extra talented."

"Extra special."

"Extra—"

"Okaaay," Ari said, holding up her hands. "You guys are extra crazy and extra certifiable."

"Is that any way to talk to your favorite aunt?" I asked her.

Ari rolled her eyes as she left the room.

I glanced at Gilly. "That girl isn't telling me anything tonight. She is in a mood."

"Welcome to my life." She put her hands on her hips. "So you'll pick me up around seven? Traffic is going to be a pain in the ass."

Speaking of pains in the ass. "I hope Gio stays in the kitchen. I wouldn't mind getting through the evening without seeing his dumb face."

"His dumb, handsome face," Gilly amended.

"His ugly insides make him ugly on the outside," I said.

"Tell that to Ted Bundy." She smiled as she put her hand on my arm. "Don't worry about me, Nora. I'm not stupid enough to give Gio another chance. I'm done with letting men like him and Lloyd walk all over me. But I do want to talk to him about Ari. I feel like something happened in Vegas, and Gio knows what it is."

"You think a man who hasn't paid attention to his daughter for ten years is going to have miraculously noticed an actual problem?"

"I'm desperate, Nora."

"Yeah, I hear you." I shook my head. "Momma bear in action."

Gilly sighed wistfully. "I do miss his food."

"But that's all."

She held up her hands. "That's definitely all."

I raised my brows at her.

"Honest," she said. "I wouldn't touch Giovanni with a ten-foot noodle."

"Don't you mean a ten-inch noodle dick?"

She giggled. "More like six inches, if I'm being honest."

"Ew, gross, Mom," Ari said as she walked back into the kitchen.

I chuckled. "Yeah, Mom."

Ari flashed me a grin.

I winked at her. "I got you." I used our moment of solidarity to ask, "So, how was Vegas?"

"Bright," she replied. "And hot."

"Sounds scintillating," I said.

She rolled her eyes. "Soooo scintillating."

Gilly made herself busy over by the sink, pretending to ignore Ari and me.

"Did you see any shows?" I asked. Gilly had told me that Ari had texted her about going to see Cirque Du Soleil, and it felt like a safe topic of conversation.

"A few," she shrugged. "It wasn't my thing."

Wow, I'd seen a Cirque show, and it was flippin' awesome. "That's too bad. I'm sorry you didn't have a better time. Did you and Marco do anything fun?"

"I guess." She sat down next to me and took a drink of her mom's tea. "The wax museum was chill, and Dad took us to see the fountain from *Ocean's Eleven* one night."

"Nice," I said. "Did you take any pictures?"

"Some." She pulled her phone from her pocket and woke up the screen. "Here's Marco posing with the wax figure of Drake."

I grabbed my reading glasses from my purse and put them on. Marco was holding a pose with his arms out and hands curled in. His smile was relaxed and genuine. I loved seeing him letting go. Marco was fantastic, but like Ari, sometimes he was wound a little too tightly.

Gilly had meandered over, slowly, as though Ari might run away if startled. She craned her neck to get a peek at the pics. I reached out and nudged Ari's phone in her mom's direction.

"That's that singer, right?" Gilly asked.

I had no idea. "Is he?"

Gilly put her reading glasses on and peered closer. "I can't believe that's a wax figure. It looks so realistic."

"Duh. That's the point, Mom." She chuckled and it made me smile. "Here's one of Marco kissing Nicki Minaj."

Gilly's eyes widened. "Is she on her hands and knees?"

"You don't even want to see the photos I deleted." Ari moved on to the next photo of herself posed in a way that made her look like she was holding up Miley Cyrus on a wrecking ball. In the background, Marco looked like he was chatting up a non-wax girl.

"I bet. Personally, I'm glad we didn't have camera phones when we were your age," I said to Ari.

"Amen, sister." Gilly held her hand up and I high-fived her. "I don't need any of my past misdeeds showing up like bad pennies."

"What does that even mean?" Ari asked.

"Google it," Gilly said.

"In other words, you don't know," Ari jabbed with a smile to take off the sting. She was already using the browser on her phone to search the phrase's origin. "People used to counterfeit pennies. What's the point in that? It's a penny."

"They used to be worth more," I said.

Ari faked wide-eyed shock. "When you were young? Back in the eighteen-eighties?"

I narrowed my gaze on the teen. "Ari, you're my favorite goddaughter. I'd hate to have to throat punch you."

She laughed hard at that. Ari's joy put a smile on Gilly's face that made the ouch from the ageist joke totally worth it.

Ari closed the browser and reopened the pictures. She swiped past the wax Miley picture to one of her and Marco posing with Giovanni in front of the MGM Grand sign. She flipped her phone over and set it on the counter facedown.

"That's all the good ones," she said.

"Thank you for showing us the pictures. They were cool."

She frowned. "Yeah, cool."

"Are you okay?"

She stared at her phone and nodded.

"What's going on, Ari?"

The girl stood up and shoved her phone back in her pocket. "Nothing."

Gilly put her elbows on the counter. "You know you can tell me anything, right?"

"Mom, there's nothing to tell. Gawd. Stop hovering."

I held out my arms for a hug. "Don't be mean," I chided gently. "Come."

Ari walked into me and put her face against my shoulder. "I really am okay, Aunt Nora," she mumbled.

I wrapped my arms around her. "I really am glad." I inhaled her scent, a combination of wintergreen, from the gum she liked so much, and strawberry from her hair gel.

"Help me set up the camera," a guy says, his voice soft and youthful.

"Are you sure you want to do this?" a girl asks. "Wouldn't it be easier to do this face-to-face?" I recognize Ari's voice, hair, and clothing, even though it's not what she's wearing right now, as she stands in front of a mirror in a bedroom predominantly blue.

"No," he says. "I've tried. I almost told them last night over chicken casserole, but I chickened out." He chuckles. "Get it? Chicken casserole, chickened out."

I see him now. His face is a blur like most faces in these strange visions. His short hair is shaved on the sides with a crop of curls up top. Similar to Ari's in cut without the fifties flip style. He's smoking something at a small open window.

Unusually loud footsteps. "Your mom," Ari says.

The young man puts out what looks to be a joint with his fingertips and waves his hands out the window. "Quick. Throw me some gum."

Ari pulls an unopened packet of wintergreen chewing gum from her pockets.

As the memory ended, I sniffed again. I didn't smell pot or cigarette smoke, and in the vision, she'd been wearing different clothing.

Ari raised her eyes suspiciously. "Don't be weird, Aunt Nora."

"Being weird is part of my charm," I told her. "Hey, do you have any gum?"

She frowned at me but took out an open packet of

wintergreen gum with only two sticks left. "I always have gum." She handed me one.

"Thanks." I smiled. "You know we're here for you, right?"

"I know." Ari shrugged. "Can I go now?"

"Yep."

When Ari got to the kitchen archway, she turned to her mom. "What's for dinner tonight?"

Gilly grimaced. "I'm going out to dinner with Nora."

"Where? Maybe you can pick something up for me."

If my best friend's body language could be described as a sound, it would have been an anguished groan. "Players."

"Mom. No. Ew. Please don't tell me you are actually falling for Dad's bullshit?"

"Ari! Language."

"Is called for," she said. I didn't disagree.

"I'm not going there to *see* your dad. Trust me, it's the last thing I want," Gilly said reassuringly.

Ari didn't look convinced. "Why did he have to come back here? Gah!" And with that, she stormed out of the room.

"So, do you want some lasagna?" Gilly called after her.

A distant upstairs door slam served as the answer.

"I think that's a yes," I said. I was relieved that Ari didn't want her mom back with her dad. "At least you don't have to worry about your kids trying to parent trap you."

"Ha ha," she said. "You're not funny."

"A little bit," I said. "On that note, I'm going to go home and get ready for dinner."

She waved her hand in front of her nose as though smelling something stank. "I've been meaning talk to you..."

"Har har." I tucked my glasses away, gathered my purse, and gave her a playful elbow. "Now who's the comedian?"

CHAPTER 9

*E*ven though Ari's memory had felt recent, I debated in my mind whether it was fair to invade the teenager's privacy. The camera thing had been unsettling, but it sounded like the boy was recording a confession, not anything that involved Ari, and while I'd seen him smoking pot, Ari had been on the other side of the room. Besides, kids sometimes experimented with pot. After all, Gilly and I had both done some recreational toking in the eighties. Still, the biggest problem was that I just didn't have enough information about the situation. The tone of the memory hadn't felt sinister. It had been more, I don't know, anxious.

Ari hadn't confided in me. Still, I felt the need to address the pot-smoking, camera-wielding elephant in the room. Fiona's death and history with drugs was making me imagine the worst, and I needed to know, for Ari and Gilly's sake. After dinner, I'd have a talk with the girl. Ari was aware of my gift, even if she'd never seen it in action, so she would just have to forgive me for invading her brain.

Portman's on the Lake Resort was located on five hundred scenic acres on Garden Cove Lake. The main hotel had twelve floors, with over two-thousand rooms, two floors for conventions, an extensive boat dock with marina, day spa, boutique and gift shops, four pools, and two bistros and a coffee shop. Players, the pride and joy of Portman's, was located on the first floor, not far from the lobby entrance.

The huge parking lot was packed, so I opted for valet parking. It was easier than trying to find a spot in this zoo of a weekend.

When we got inside to the restaurant, Twyla led us across the dining room to our table.

"This isn't so bad," Gilly said.

A large man's butt brushed the back of my chair as he made a brief apology and scooted past me toward the men's room.

I nodded. "At least it's nowhere near the kitchen, so we have less of a chance of accidentally running into Gio. Besides, we didn't come for the ambiance."

The restaurant was packed with patrons. Not an empty seat in the house, even the bar seating was full. The Italian music pumping through speakers could barely be heard over the rumble of conversations.

"This restaurant is hopping." I glanced around. I'd only eaten at Players once before, and I'd thought the food was okay but pricey. I saw a few locals, including Big Don and his wife, Claire. Big Don was, as his name suggested, big. He was six feet five inches tall, and before settling down in Garden Cove well before my time, he'd played college ball at a big school. Claire had been a local celebrity and beauty queen. She was now in her seventies, but thanks to good genes and probably a good plastic surgeon, she was still stunning. She had chocolate-brown hair, glossy with shine and highlights that brightened her face. Her eyelashes were thick and long, most likely false, but who cared, they made her eyes pop. My mother used to say that Claire never met a stranger. I didn't know her or Big Don well, but they'd came to both my parents' funerals, and I had a lot of respect for them.

Across from Big Don sat a man I recognized from the night before. The guy the pharmacist, Burt Adler, had briefly met with outside of Sully's. Tonight, he wore a suit and tie, his curls slicked back. The woman next to him had dyed-blonde hair, a little overprocessed and styled in waves. She smiled at Claire, her lips noticeably thick and misshapen with filler, as they chatted.

"Who's that with Big Don and his wife?" I asked Gilly.

She shook her head. "You really don't pay attention to what goes on in town, do you?"

Gilly wasn't wrong. I'd lived in the city long enough that I wasn't interested in people who didn't impact my life. Other than the occasional wave, my neighbors and I never even stopped to introduce ourselves. "Just tell me who it is."

"Jameson Campbell. The woman is his wife, Lucy. They moved into town about eighteen years ago and bought Garden Cove Lake Condos."

"Those are the condominiums out on forty-four near Sully's Surf and Turf, right?"

"Yes."

"I saw that Campbell guy last night in the parking lot at Sully's. He was talking to the pharmacist."

"Were they fighting or something?"

"No, nothing like that." I shrugged. "They spoke for a minute or two before Adler left. But I got a strange vibe from them, is all."

"Like a smell-o-vibe?"

"No. Just a regular ol' skin-crawling sensation."

"Huh. Well, maybe they're just friends."

"Burt Adler is also friends with Phil, remember?"

"Trying not to. Man, I'm starving." Gilly put on her glasses. She blinked then gave me a *holy crap* look. "It looks like the prices match the demand here," she said as she studied the one-page menu. "Cripes, you'd think the cheese was laced with gold."

"Dinner's on me," I told her.

"Was it ever a question?" She blew me a kiss. "So, how are you planning to handle this psychic investigation of yours?"

"There are so many people here." The scent of marinara, garlic, cheeses, and yeasty breads permeated the room. "And so many smells. I have no idea what I should do."

"Reese is right. You helped clear my name, and you helped my neighbor solve the case of his missing daughter. I hate to say it, but you're a natural."

"I was operating on pure desperation and perspiration. I would have turned over every rock in this town to clear your name."

"Awww." Her lower lip jutted as she touched her chest with her fingers. "I would do the same for you."

I grinned at her. "Good to know."

"Let's make a game plan."

"Okay, Coach. Do you need a whistle and a playbook?"

She gave me a flat stare. "Can you be serious?"

"I *am* being serious. Give me some ideas where I should start."

A petite, twenty-something waitress with pin-straight blonde hair approached our table. "Hello. I'm Clara, your server." She had a bright, wide smile and pleasant eyes. "We're upgrading your table. Would you follow me?"

"We're okay sitting here," I said as another butt scooted past my chair. I looked around the room full of diners. "Besides, we don't want to wait for a better table to order."

"No waiting," Clara said. She crossed her heart. "Promise."

Gilly and I reluctantly followed our happy-go-lucky server. When she took us to a swinging door that said *employees only*, several alarm bells sounded in my head.

She offered a reassuring, "It's just this way," and ushered Gilly and me on through to the kitchen.

A sound of dismay escaped Gilly when we saw Gio, wearing a black chef's jacket and matching hat, standing next to a table three feet or so from all the cooking action.

FOR WHOM THE SMELL TOLLS

"It's our chef's table," Clara said, delighted.

"I can see that," I said.

"Chef Rossi would like you to be his guests for dinner tonight."

Gio rushed around the table to Gilly's side and pulled a chair out for her as one of his cooks—a burly young man in a white chef's jacket with black trim, and the name Chad embroidered above a right breast pocket—offered me the same courtesy.

"Thanks," I said, my focus on Gilly and Gio, and Gilly's response to Gio's gallantry. To my relief, my BFF looked as astonished and annoyed as I felt.

"I saw that Nora had a reservation, so I'd hoped you were her plus one," he said to Gilly. "I'm so pleased you've come."

"I'm not here for you," she said.

I gave her a mental fist bump.

Gio smiled. "Clara is going to take good care of you both."

"It's up to you, Gilly. I'm happy enough to go back out to our reserved table."

"We can stay. Unless you like having butts and groins brushing your back all night."

Being so close to the bathrooms had been unfortunate, but I know Twyla did her best. It's a wonder there were any tables available at all. "Okay. We'll stay."

Clara set menus in front of us then cleared her throat. "Our new chef, Giovanni Rossi, a James Beard nominee and Michelin Rising Star award winner, has invited you to experience a culinary journey of Italy as he takes you from," she glanced at Gio nervously then continued, "our selection of *antipasto* and *insalate* to our *piato principale* or our featured *bisteca*." Her pronunciation of each Italian word was stiff but precise. She'd obviously been practicing.

When Gio gave her an approving nod, she continued, "Then to complete the tour of Italy, you will finish with your choice of a deliciously rich tiramisu, traditional *crème brûlée*, or *Cannoli di Rossi*, the chef's special of the night. It features chocolate-dipped cannoli stuffed with a cinnamon-and-almond-infused sweet ricotta and topped with crushed candied almonds. For the chocolate lovers, we have a bittersweet chocolate and raspberry flourless cake served with our homemade vanilla and raspberry swirl gelato." She finished with a triumphant smile.

My disdain for Gio had nothing to do with Clara— or his ability to cook amazing meals—so I nodded approvingly. "It all sounds yummy."

"Can I start your dinner off with some wine?"

"Absolutely," Gilly said. Her tart gaze landed on Gio. "A Zinfandel. And I'm gonna need the whole bottle."

I raised both brows at Gilly.

She raised one back. "You're driving."

I smirked. A tipsy Gilly was prone to fighting, and the way she was glaring at her ex, it wasn't going to take much for her to waylay him. I looked at Clara "I'll take an iced tea."

I watched as a pleased smile spread across Gio's smug face. "So nice to have you here, Gillian. I wanted you to come to my opening night, but I dared not hope."

"Our being here has nothing to do with you," I reiterated.

He scoffed. "I find that hard to believe. Even so," he softened his gaze as he looked at my BFF, "I hope you'll stay for me."

"Do you have bail money, Nora?" Gilly asked me while holding Gio's stare. "Because I think I'm going to need it."

"Yep. I got you covered."

Gio laughed, the sound rich and melodious. "Ah, Gillian. I'm glad to see you haven't lost your wonderful sense of humor."

"I'm not kidding," she said flatly.

He didn't stop smiling. I'd forgotten Gio's ego was the size of a small galaxy. I honestly don't think he comprehended that Gilly was serious. Nope. In his narcissistic mind, she was being coy and cute.

"Don't you have cooking to do?" I asked.

He ignored me. "I hope you'll try the *filleto al gorgonzola*. It is particularly good, and one of your favorites, if I remember correctly."

Gilly made a show of looking at the menu. "I'm in the mood for lobster ravioli."

"You mean the *ravioli aragosta*," he said.

Gilly put the menu down. "I said what I said."

The side of his mouth quirked up. "So, you want the lobster ravioli?" Cripes. The man was amused. Did he think Gilly was flirting with him?

"Can you give us a minute?" I said to Gio. "I'd like some time to look over the appetizers."

The pretentious bastard didn't bother to correct me.

He gave a small flourish with his hand then nodded. "Of course. Please take your time. You are my guests."

When he walked away from the small table, I fixed my gaze on Gilly.

She didn't flinch. "What?"

"You know what."

"There's a reason I married the man in the first place."

"And there's a reason you divorced him."

"And there's a reason I'm staying divorced." She thinned her lips. "Stop giving me the evil eye. I'm not planning to fall back into Gio's arms, Nora. I don't know how many times I have to say it. Give me some credit, okay?"

"You deserve a man who will move planets to be with you. Gio wasn't willing to stay in the same orbit as you and the kids." I jerked my thumb toward Gio. "He will always put himself first."

"I know that, Nora." She picked up her menu, effectively ending our current conversation. "I think I'm going to start with artichoke bruschetta."

Okay, then. Message received. "I'll get the shrimp scampi, and we can share."

She forced a smile that didn't reach her eyes. "Deal."

It was a start. At least she was trying to forgive me for my pushy overprotectiveness. Maybe the need to protect people from themselves hadn't just been my ex-husband's flaw. "I'm sorry," I said. "You're a grown-ass woman, and you don't need a lecture from me."

"I *am* a grown-ass woman," she agreed. Her eyes softened. "But I'm glad I have you in my corner. I know you'll always fight for me." She glanced meaningfully at Gio. "I'm not a fool, Nora. He's charming and gorgeous, and I'll admit, I am not immune to it. I loved him enough to marry him and give him children. That kind of love doesn't just disappear. But I will never trust him again. So, no matter how much I might want for things to be different, for Gio to be a different man, I'll never forgive him for what he did to our family."

She was throwing out a lot of *nevers*, but all I could think about was the love not disappearing. I didn't want Gilly to hate her ex-douchebag because that was giving him too much emotional space in her heart. I wanted her to say she was indifferent to the man. Indifference was the bane of love and hate. Indifference allowed a person to move on.

Clara arrived back at our table with a bottle of Zinfandel, two wine glasses, and a tall iced tea. She made a show of pouring a small amount into a glass before handing it to Gilly to test.

"I'm sure it's fine," Gilly told her. "Just give me a good pour."

Clara's eyes bugged. She was trying to impress her new boss, and Gilly was not making it easy. "Of course." She tipped the bottle and poured until the glass was three-quarters full. She looked at me. "I've brought you a glass in case you want to share."

Gilly smiled. "Have a little, Nora. One glass isn't going to get you drunk, and it will pair nicely with the shrimp scampi."

"Fine. Just a little, though."

Clara's smile widened. "Excellent." She only gave me

two fingers worth then set the bottle down. "What would you like to start with?"

"Shrimp scampi and artichoke bruschetta," Gilly said.

"Great choices. And for the *piata principale?*"

I would have ordered a carbonara, but it wasn't on the menu. "I'll take the chicken pesto tortellini for my main dish."

"And I'll have the *ravioli aragosta,*" Gilly said, using the Italian for lobster ravioli now that Gio wasn't around. "Can you bring extra fresh-grated parmesan to the table as well?"

"Definitely." She finished writing our order. "I'll take your dessert order when I bring out your entree. Is there anything else I can get you?"

I'd come to the restaurant to ask about Fiona, and now seemed as good a time as any to get started. "Hey, I'm so sorry to hear about the server you guys lost yesterday. Fiona McKay, right?"

Clara stiffened. "Yes, that was a shame. Fiona worked here for a long time."

I nodded sympathetically but noticed Clara didn't seem too broken up about it. "Were you two close?"

"Not really." Her eyes darted toward the cooks and back to me. "I really shouldn't be talking about this," Clara said, then lowered her voice to a whisper. "She quit a few days ago. It really left us in a lurch. Especially with a new chef. Chef Rossi has been such a good teacher, though. We're lucky to have him."

"Lucky," I repeated then pivoted back to Fiona. "Was Fiona seeing anyone?"

Clara widened her eyes then shook her head. "I should really put in this order for you."

The room was full of strong food scents, but nothing that was triggering a memory for Clara. Even so, I could tell the server knew something more she wasn't saying.

I scanned the kitchen. Chad, the cook who'd pulled out my chair, was paying a lot of attention to our conversation.

I dove in with my next comment to gauge Clara and Chad's reactions. "I'm the one who found her. I pulled Fiona's body out of the lake."

Clara clasped her order pad to her chest, her mouth dropped open, and her gaze skittered to Chad, whose cheeks turned redder than the marinara sauce he stirred. He dropped the spoon onto the counter and stared at me, his eyes clouding with a mixture of something akin to fear and anger.

He left his station and headed toward the back. "I'm taking a break," he said. "Five minutes."

An older man moved from cutting vegetables to Chad's station and picked up his spoon to continue stirring the pot.

I caught Clara's arm before she could get away. "I hope I didn't upset you."

Overwhelming scents of earthy beef and garlicky marinara took me under.

Lights illuminate the mostly empty parking lot. A woman walks toward an orange four-door hatchback. It's chilly, and the wind bites at her face. The moon half-hidden by large, dark clouds, like a storm is coming. She spies a man and a woman in front of a blue truck and increases her pace.

"I have to go," the woman says. Her dark hair is pulled back in a ponytail, and even with the parking lot lights, I can't tell the exact color.

"Why do you want to leave?" he says. "Your whole life is here. What about your family?"

"They'll be glad I'm not around to embarrass them."

"What about me?" His voice is full of sorrow and ache. "I love you."

"I can't stay in Garden Cove anymore," she says. She places a hand on her stomach. "I have too much to lose if I stay. Come with me, Chad. I'll have enough money in ten days to support us both until we can find our own way." She moves her hand from her belly to his chest. "Together."

"You know I can't leave right now. I'm on probation."

"You can run. We'll go to Mexico. You'll be free too."

When he doesn't respond, Fiona says, "Ten days. If you change your mind, tell me."

The woman walking toward them stumbles, pitching forward. She loses her grip on the takeout box she's holding. The box bursts as it hits the ground and spills the spaghetti with marinara sauce.

Clara extracted her arm from my grasp and looked at me oddly. "Please, excuse me. I need to put your order in."

The moment the waitress walked away, I looked at Gilly.

"Did you see something?" she asked.

"Yes."

Fiona had been seeing Chad, long enough for him to

declare his love. Was he aware of her drug habits? The only way I would find out was to ask. I looked toward where Chad had disappeared out the back.

I stood up from the table and put my cloth napkin on my seat. "I think I need some fresh air."

CHAPTER 10

*C*had stood outside the back door of the kitchen at the bottom of the steps. He had a lit cigarette in one shaking hand, flicking a lighter on then off with the other.

I approached with the caution I'd have exercised with a wild animal. I cleared my throat to alert him to my presence. He stared off at the clear, starry sky, unaware of me. I noticed the speaker buds in his ears. No wonder he didn't hear me.

My knees didn't love stairs, so I used the rail as I took the four steps to the bottom one at a time until I was standing behind him. Luckily, a bright lamp anchored above the door offered plenty of light for me to see. I tapped on Chad's shoulder.

He swung around, his eyes hard, his body tensed for a fight.

When he saw it was me, his eyes remained wary, but his shoulders and arms relaxed. He removed the earbuds, putting them into his pocket. He took a long drag off his cigarette and, after he blew out a large cloud of smoke, he said, "You shouldn't be out here."

"I'm sorry I'm interrupting your break. I couldn't help but notice you were upset when I asked about Fiona. Did you know her well?" I wondered if Chad would be honest.

"I met her four months ago when I started working here, and we were on most shifts together." His voice was thick and hoarse. The lamp made the wetness in his eyes sparkle. "Yeah, I knew her," he said.

"I'm so sorry."

He shrugged, took another drag, then flicked the lit cigarette out into the employee lot. Glowing orange bits scattered when it hit the ground. "You were there, huh? You found her?"

"Yes," I told him. "I was getting some air down by the water when I...saw her."

"They say she drowned."

I nodded. "From what I know, it's true." Shawn had said there was water in her lungs.

He shook his head. "Fiona loved the water. She was even scuba certified, or whatever they call that." His stare grew distant as if thinking of better times. "I swear the girl was born with gills. It's hard to believe she drowned."

Chad's praise of Fiona's swimming ability lined up with Reese's. Still, it didn't mean her death wasn't an accident. It simply could have been a tragic irony.

"I'm friends with Fiona's cousin. You might know her. Reese McKay. She's a police officer here in Garden Cove."

113

"I know who she is. Fiona introduced me once when her cousin came into the restaurant. She used to go on about Reese being the only person she could trust." He glanced away. "Besides me."

"The news must have been a shock," I said. "How long were you two a couple?"

He gave me a sharp look. "We weren't. Not really. We were friends. I...I just..."

I knew from seeing Clara's memory that they were more than just friends. "You loved her."

His whole body clenched, his shoulders almost rising to his ears. "You have to understand. Fiona was like the north star for me. She felt like the way home. Until she didn't." He crossed his large arms over his chest in a hug. "Christ, I need a meeting."

"A meeting?"

He huffed, and the pungent aroma of black coffee and stale cigarette smoke surrounded me.

"The program works if you just keep working it," a man says. His face is unclear, but I can't miss the tattoos on his arms and neck. It's Pippa's guy, Jordy Hines. "I've been clean for twelve years," he says.

"Does it get easier?" a woman asks. I recognize her thick auburn hair. Fiona McKay. She's popping a rubber band against her left wrist. "I mean, will I get to a point where I don't want the drugs anymore?" She drops her hand to her belly. "I need to stay clean now."

"I wish addiction worked like that." Jordy chuckles softly. "I still have days when I miss the high." He takes a drink of coffee then leans forward and puts his elbows on his knees. "Honestly, I can go weeks, months even, without jonesing for

the obliteration, but then sometimes it's a daily struggle. But that's what meetings are for. That's what a sponsor is for."

A guy sitting next to the girl says, "I've been sober for two years. Meetings work." It's not hard to make out that it's Chad. He places his hand over Fiona's red, whelped wrist. I notice a scar, thick and at least two inches long, under the whelp.

When I came back from the memory, Chad was staring at me. "I better get back inside," he said.

"Wait." I straightened my shoulders. "Fiona had drugs in her system when she died. Do you know where she would have gotten them?"

"No." He shook his head. "That's not possible. Fiona has been clean for months now. She wouldn't." He scratched his head then jammed his lighter into his pocket. "She wouldn't be on drugs."

"What makes you so sure?" I reached out and touched his arm. "Is it because she was pregnant?"

"How did you..." He stared me, frowning. " She didn't tell anyone. Just me."

All the belly touching in the visions had been a big hint. Gilly was like that when she was pregnant with the twins, always rubbing her stomach. "How far along was she?"

"Almost three months," Chad said, his eyes full of sorrow.

Fiona's DUI had occurred two and a half months ago. I wondered if it happened before she knew she was pregnant. "Were you the father?"

"No." He heaved a sigh. "But I would have taken care of her and the baby as if it were my own."

"Who then?"

115

His expression was raw with loss. "I don't know. She wouldn't tell me. Now, I've really got to go." He gave me a wide birth as he walked around me and went up the steps to the door. At the top stair, he turned to me. "Fiona was smart and funny and gentle. She's the kind of person who picked up turtles to help them cross the road so they wouldn't get run over. She left cat food out for strays in the trailer park where I live, and she captured spiders and took them outside. She had her troubles, but she was a good person."

I nodded, emotion choking my throat. "Thank you for telling me," I said.

He went inside without another word.

My encounter with Chad left me with a few answers and so many more questions. She'd been in Narcotics Anonymous and she'd been pregnant. Had that been in the medical examiner's report? This added a whole new level of complication surrounding Fiona McKay, and it begged the question—where was she expecting to get all the money to move out of town? And why was she in such a hurry?

Also, that scar on Fiona's wrist. Even when I'd found her, she'd worn a wide cuff bracelet on her left wrist. Was it to hide the scar? Had she attempted suicide in the past? Did Reese know? She hadn't said Fiona was suicidal.

Could Fiona have drowned herself as a way to escape whatever trouble she was in? And was that trouble related to drugs or to her secret pregnancy? Or both?

Also, Jordy was in NA. So many flippin' revelations

from one little vision. Did Pippa know her man was a recovering addict? The meetings were supposed to be anonymous, but I couldn't take the knowledge back. Did it matter if Pip knew? He was sober now and had been for twelve years, but I couldn't shake his words. *I still have days when I miss the high.*

* * *

THE *ANTIPASTO* HAD ARRIVED by the time I returned to the table. Gio stood over Gilly, his hand on the back of her chair as they chatted. She was nodding and not screaming. I wasn't sure how I felt about the pleasantries going on between them, but again, I had to remind myself that it wasn't my life.

I sat down and Gio excused himself.

The scampi was in a small cast iron serving platter, and the jumbo shrimp were still sizzling.

"It's hot," Gilly said as she picked up a piece of bruschetta spread with artichoke dip and melting cheese.

"Thanks. That looks good."

"It's heaven," she sighed. She took a bite. "Mmm-mmm." Cheese strings bridged the gap between her mouth and the bread. "So good," she mumbled.

"I can see that." I laughed. The shrimp was cooked to perfection. Plump, juicy, and tender. I hated how good it tasted. I mean, I loved a great meal, but a calculated part of me wanted to see Gio fail miserably.

"So." Gilly leaned in conspiratorially. "Did you find out anything?"

"A few things," I said quietly. "I think Fiona tried to kill herself at one time. There was a scar on her left wrist that looked too deliberate to be an accident."

"Did your smell-o-vision show you a memory of her cutting herself?"

"No. She was attending Narcotics Anonymous. Chad says she's been clean for two months."

"I wonder if she was on drugs when she drowned?"

I knew Fiona had drugs in her when she'd drowned, but I wanted to keep my promise to Shawn to not divulge what he'd told me in confidence. "Maybe. She could have relapsed."

"Anything else?"

"Yes, but I'll tell you on the ride home," I said. I would tell her about the pregnancy, but I would keep Jordy's stuff to myself. His sobriety was his business and his alone. I wouldn't violate that.

I couldn't shake the scar on Fiona's wrist. At this point, I was wondering if the girl hadn't taken her own life. Pregnant drug addict who can't stay clean. She'd sounded upset on the phone message. Desperate. It wasn't a stretch to go from accidental drowning to suicide. If that was the case, then her call to Reese could have been a final cry for help. If true, the news would devastate Reese even more.

"Are you okay?" Gilly asked.

"I'm worried that whatever I find out for Reese is going to make Fiona's death even harder for her."

* * *

GILLY HAD POLISHED off three glasses of wine, and we were both full from an amazing dinner. We took our tiramisu in to-go boxes, along with the lasagna meals Gio boxed up for the twins...*on the house.* I figured a free meal at his fancy restaurant was the least Gio owed his ex-wife. Had I known he was going to foot the bill, I might have ordered an extra dessert.

It hurt my heart to see how Gio was so adept at publicly playing the doting dad when it suited him, which hadn't been often in the past ten years. I also didn't like the idea that he could sweep into town and try to wipe away the decade of struggle and rebuilding Gilly had done to find a new normal for her and the kids.

On the way out of the restaurant, I brushed against a man waiting by the hostess table.

I had to clench my teeth to keep my mouth from dropping open. Phil Williams was looking at me the same way I'd looked at my tiramisu. Yuck.

"Oh, hey. I didn't get your name—" He stopped talking when he saw Gilly behind me, his eyes narrowing at my friend.

Then he fixed his gaze back on me, his expression turning from pleasant to pissed-off. "You're Nora Black."

I didn't get a chance to say anything else because Gilly pushed me from behind and kept us moving until we were out the door.

I handed my ticket to the guy manning the valet stand.

"That mother...*fluffer.*" Gilly was shaking so hard,

the bag of to-go boxes rattled in her hands. She cast a quick look over her shoulder. "He's not following us."

"He better not," I said, though I didn't feel nearly as tough as I sounded. I breathed a sigh of relief as the valet arrived with my car. "C'mon, Gilly," I said. "Let's get out of here."

CHAPTER 11

"That's terrible, Nora," Gilly said after I told her about what I'd learned from Chad. "That poor girl was pregnant? I'm just…I don't even know how to react."

"I get it. I'm in shock, too." We were a few blocks from Gilly's house and my car was filling up with the robust garlic and cilantro scents of lasagna. "Even though Chad wasn't the father, I got the impression he would've moved the moon to be with Fiona. If she'd managed to leave—they might've had a chance."

"Why leave, though?" asked Gilly. "If Fiona was getting her crap together, why wouldn't she tell her parents? Jenny McKay doesn't seem like the type of woman who would turn her daughter out. And with a baby on the way and a new commitment to sobriety, she might've been fine here, too."

I shook my head. "My guess? Something to do with the pregnancy. Maybe the sperm donor wasn't thrilled."

"But you didn't get any smell-confirmation of the baby daddy?"

"Not even a whiff. Your guess is as good as mine." I sighed.

"I'll keep my ear to the ground. I know a lot of people at Portman's. Someone there might know who Fiona had been seeing before she took up with Chad. Remember? I told you my friend Natalie runs the spa there, and she used to work with me at the Rose Palace. I'll start with her. People are always confiding in their massage therapists."

"Thanks, Gils. That's a big help."

When we got to Gilly's, I parked and went inside with her. I still had to chat with a certain teenage girl. "I'll go up and tell the twins the food's here."

Gilly, who was singing Pat Benatar's "Hit Me With Your Best Shot," nodded and danced her way into the kitchen. My back was stiff from the drive, and the ibuprofen I popped before dinner was barely taking the edge off the muscle ache. I regretted volunteering to go up the stairs, knowing that what goes up must also come down, and my knees and my back wouldn't thank me for the effort.

I heard music coming from Ari's room. Her closed door had a sign that said, "Enter without knocking at your own risk."

I heeded the warning and knocked. The music's volume lowered.

"What do you want?" she asked.

"To talk," I said. "And we've brought you back some food."

The door opened before I finished saying food. "Sorry, Aunt Nora. I thought you were Mom or Marco."

Marco peeked his head out of his room. He looked disheveled, like he'd just woken up from a nap.

"There's lasagna in the kitchen," I told him.

He rubbed his face. "Cool," he said. "Be right there."

After he ducked back into his room, I said to Ari, "Can I talk to you alone for a moment?"

"Uhm, sure," she said. She opened her door wider. "The room is a mess."

I looked around as I stepped inside. There were a few clothes on her lounge chair near her window, her bed was unmade, and there was half a cup of some drink on her computer desk. Other than that, the bedroom was pretty clean. "What a pigsty," I teased.

She grinned. "It's messy for me."

"I'll give you that," I said.

I sat down on the edge of her bed. She took the cue and dragged her computer chair over and sat across from me.

She waited for me to speak first. I wasn't sure where to start, so I just jumped in. "You know about my...sense of smell. How it can sometimes show me memories?"

Ari blinked but didn't say anything.

"You know, other people's memories," I explained.

"Okaaay," she said slowly. "And?"

"When we hugged earlier, I smelled wintergreen gum."

"I always have wintergreen gum." Ari shrugged, her eyes darting toward the door as if she were planning her escape.

"Yes, but when I smelled it, I saw you in a blue bedroom with a guy." I took a deep breath, bolstering my courage. "He was asking you to set up a camera. You sounded worried."

"Gawd, Aunt Nora." She stood up and took a few steps back, visibly upset.

"I wasn't trying to get into your business. I can't control when my ability kicks in and when it doesn't. It's tied to strong emotions, so I know whatever I saw was important. That boy...he wasn't making you...you know, do something you didn't want to do?"

"Like what?" she asked. Her eyes narrowed at me when I didn't answer right away. "Wow, Aunt Nora. We weren't making sex tapes if that's what you're worried about."

"I won't lie and say it didn't cross my mind," I told her. "Briefly."

"Did you tell my mom?"

"I haven't said anything yet. And you can be mad at me, but I love you, Ari. You are the closest thing I will ever have to a daughter of my own, and I want you happy and safe. What I saw in the vision didn't feel safe."

She sighed and plunked back down in the chair. "It wasn't anything bad, Aunt Nora. I promise."

"Will you tell me what was going on?"

"The camera wasn't for me. Johnny wanted to make a coming-out video for his parents, and he'd wanted to do it before I left for Las Vegas. He didn't have the nerve to tell them in person, and he wanted help with the recording. So, I helped. That's all."

Ten kinds of relief washed over me. Well, I guess that answered the question about whether Johnny was a romantic interest for Ari. "And that's all?"

"Yes, that's it. I swear," she said.

"What about the pot?" I asked.

She cringed. "You saw that, too, huh?"

"Yep."

"Johnny smokes it for anxiety."

"Prescription?"

"No," Ari admitted. "But I don't smoke it, Aunt Nora. I tried once. That was enough. It burned the crap out of my throat, and I didn't like the way it clouded my head."

"I think you should tell your mom about the experimenting with marijuana," I said, knowing it was something I couldn't and wouldn't keep from Gilly.

"It was last year, and I already did. I told her the next day." Ari grimaced. "I'm surprised she didn't tell you."

I was surprised, too, but the fact that Gilly already knew lifted a weight from my shoulders. "Okay," I said. "How did his coming out go? Your mood when you got home tonight tells me it might not have gone too well."

"He hasn't given it to them." She shook her head. "That's not why I'm in a mood."

"It's Vegas, right? Something happened there."

Her eyes widened. "Did you get another vision?"

"No. You looked miserable the other night when your dad brought you all home."

She hugged her arms. "He's a jerk, is all. I wish he'd have stayed gone."

"Did he do something to you?" Maybe he'd yelled at her or called her Ariana one too many times. Sometimes it didn't take much to send a teenager over the edge.

"Not to me," she said. "Not exactly."

"To Marco?"

"Not to either of us." Her gaze darkened. "Can you keep a secret from my mom?"

"Probably, but I'm not super confident," I teased. "However, if it's something bad, then absolutely not. But you should tell me anyway."

Ari snorted. "I love that you don't bullshit me, Aunt Nora."

"Is that your new favorite word?"

She smirked then shook her head. "Dad was in Garden Cove three weeks ago. He stayed at Portman's on the Lake without telling any of us. Marco and I haven't seen him in three years, and he just shows up without saying a word."

"How did you find this out?"

"I overheard him talking to someone about it in Las Vegas. When I confronted him, he said he'd done it to spare Marco and me in case he didn't get the job here in town, and he hadn't wanted to get our hopes up. But he made me promise to keep it a secret from Marco and Mom." The corner of her lip curled up as she looked at me. "But he didn't tell me I had to keep it a secret from you."

A combination of anger and shock coursed through me. Gio had been in town three weeks earlier, and he hadn't even tried to see his kids. What in the world had he been thinking? Why would he try to hide it? Why make his daughter complicit in his secret? Obviously, she'd been struggling with the idea of telling her mom.

I nodded to Ari. "And since I haven't promised you to keep it to myself, you can't stop me from telling anyone I want," I said.

"Actually, I don't know why I'm struggling with this. I can't count the number of times Dad has made promises he's broken. I'll tell Mom."

I nodded. "Are you sure?"

"I am. I'll do it tonight. I'll tell her and Marco."

I scooted forward and patted her knee. "I'm proud of you." I paused, thinking about Fiona's secrets and how she hadn't been able to confide in her family. "You know that you can always tell me anything, and I mean anything at all. I will never judge you. I will support you and love you. You know that, right?"

"I do." She smiled at me. "I love you, Aunt Nora."

"The feeling is completely mutual, kiddo."

AFTER I LEFT GILLY'S, I couldn't get the events of the last two days to stop going round and round in my head like a nightmare Ferris wheel. Running into Phil at the restaurant had rattled me, and for the first time in a long while, I was afraid to be alone. Did I think the man would stalk me to my home? Probably not. He had guys for that. Like Carl Grigsby. I couldn't shake the fear.

I found myself driving out of town toward Lake Access Road V and turning down a rural road that led to the small two-bedroom cabin where Ezra lived.

It was late, but not so late that he'd be sleeping. I didn't want to wait another minute to tell him about Fiona, Reese, and Phil, and frankly, everything.

I thought about Chad saying how Reese was the only person Fiona could trust aside from himself. I understood the feeling. For a long time, I only had two people in the world I trusted completely. Gilly and Pippa were there for me no matter what, and I counted myself lucky that I had a small tribe around me. But, as my car idled on a gravel road a hundred yards from Ezra's place, I realized that I counted him among my trusted people now as well.

Was I setting myself up for a broken heart? Maybe. But I was at an age where I realized that there was no such thing as happily ever after. And even if it had existed, it was no longer a goal for me. I wanted to be happy in the present. In order to do that, I had to put aside future worry. I didn't need to know how Ezra and I would fit in ten or twenty years. We fit right now.

A sharp rap on the window startled me from my thoughts, and I yipped.

"What's going on?" Ezra said.

My heart thumped so hard I could feel it pulsing in my neck. I rolled down the window. "You scared the bejeezus out of me."

"I think that's my line." His expression was bemused. "I had someone pull down my drive, park a fair distance away, and turn off their lights as if they were watching the place. That's pretty frightening."

I opened my mouth to argue with him, but he had a solid point. "You're right. I'm sorry. I should have called you first before driving out here."

Ezra's green eyes softened as he leaned over, bracing himself on the open window frame. "You can come by anytime you want, Nora." He traced the curve of my jaw with his finger. "I hope you know you're welcome at my home."

I let out a soft *pah*. A breath I hadn't known I was holding. "God, you're easy," I said, playing on his nickname.

He smiled, and I melted. A lot.

"That's what they tell me." He stood up, and I saw he was wearing a t-shirt, sweatpants, a pair of tennis shoes, and a conceal-carry belly band over his shirt and wrapped around his waist. His pistol was snug in the holster.

I guess I *had* scared him. "You brought your gun?"

"Just in case," he said. He walked around to the passenger side of the car. I unlocked the door and he slid into the seat. He turned to me and leaned in, his warm lips moving against my mouth with a tenderness that seared me to my soul.

"Whoa," I said when he ended the kiss, his face still close to mine. "What was that for?"

He cupped my face. "God, you're beautiful."

I'm not an insecure woman, but mentally I added, *for someone over fifty*.

Ezra seemed to read my mind. "You have a light in you, Nora. A flame that can't be doused. I love that about you."

My stomach fluttered. "Thanks," I said, suddenly shy and at a loss for words.

He chuckled. "So why did you drive out here tonight and park on my road? Is it because of Fiona McKay?" He sat back in the seat. "I can't get her out of my head either. Poor kid. I interviewed her parents today. It was awful. I can't stop thinking about how I'd feel if something like that happened to Mason. A senseless tragedy."

"Horrible," I agreed. "Reese stopped by Scents and Scentsability yesterday. She's devastated. Reese doesn't think Fiona died accidentally. She's got a combo of grief and guilt in her."

"She confronted me yesterday morning," Ezra said. He raised his brow at me. "Did she play you the message?"

"Yes, she played me the phone message," I told him.

Ezra nodded. "I was going to tell you," he said. "She blames herself right now, but that will fade with time. Mourning is never simple or quick."

"Nope." I was still grieving my mother after almost a year without her. "Losing someone doesn't magically stop hurting."

Ezra took my hand. "I'm glad you came tonight. I've missed you."

"I've missed you," I said. "But it's not the only reason I drove out here."

He tipped his head to the side. "Tell me."

"I don't even know where to start."

"The beginning is always as good a place as any."

"Well, the first part, I could be overreacting. I ran into Phil Williams at the pharmacy the other day."

Ezra's back straightened as he rotated his knees toward me. "Did he threaten you?"

I shook my head. "At the time, I don't think he knew who I was. He..."

"He what?" I could almost feel the hackles rising on the back of Ezra's neck.

"He gave me his card."

"He...gave you his card? Why?"

Bile burned the back of my throat, probably because of a combination of spicy Italian food and my encounter with Williams. "He asked to take me to dinner."

Ezra bristled. "Then what happened?"

"He went into a back room with Burt Adler, the pharmacist, and I got the heck out of there. I'd only seen him that one time at the Rose Palace Resort, when he'd fired Gilly, and I guess he'd been so focused on her that he hadn't noticed me."

"Well, he's noticed you now. What else?" Ezra was using his cop voice. I recognized the tone from when he'd interviewed me after Lloyd Briscoll's death. "Tell me everything."

"Also, Fiona had been with me right before he showed up. She seemed really happy about some news and was flashing around the missing ring I told you about. But she made a hasty retreat when Phil arrived. I could be projecting my own fear onto her, but she acted scared. Then yesterday when Reese came by, she asked me to look into Fiona's death. And by look, I mean nose. She wants me to see if I can find a different reason for her cousin's drowning. She thinks Fiona wanted her to ask me."

Ezra shook his head as he picked at the hairs on his arm. "And you told her yes."

I massaged my temple. "Yes."

"Okay."

"So, tonight, I went to Players, the restaurant Fiona used to work at. It turns out she quit a few days ago." I frowned. "She'd had a thing with one of the cooks, a guy named Chad. I think she might have loved him. But, she was leaving town. I think she was getting money from someone and she planned to disappear."

"You saw this?"

"Yes. It was actually a waitress' memory. A woman named Clara. She saw a conversation out in the employee parking lot."

"Anything else?"

"Chad is a recovering addict. He said that Fiona's been clean for two months. That doesn't jive with Fiona having oxy and fentanyl in her blood when she died—"

"Did Reese tell you that?" he asked. "The autopsy report was completed this afternoon, but the chief made her take the weekend off. I wonder who told her about it."

"That part wasn't Reese." I took a deep breath and steeled my courage. I couldn't handle the knowledge about Fiona's past on my own. I needed to trust that

Ezra wouldn't overreact. My eye twitched as I reached up and gripped the steering wheel as if to steady myself as I got ready to tell him something that, as a civilian, I shouldn't know about. "Fiona was arrested four months ago for drug possession with the intent to distribute."

CHAPTER 12

*E*zra did a double take. "I would have heard about it. Did you see this in one of your scent-memory visions?"

I bit my lower lip. "That's not how I know. Shawn told me."

"Shawn?" He pulled a face. "You mean Chief Rafferty?"

"Yes," I said. "You probably didn't know about it because it happened in Rasfield, not here in Garden Cove."

He was leaning forward in his seat now, and I could see him trying to wrap his brain around what I'd told him.

"Wait. I'm confused," he said. "The chief called you to talk about Fiona McKay?"

"No, not for Fiona." I sighed. I wanted to tell Ezra it wasn't as bad as it sounded, but I think it *was* that bad, if not worse. Shawn had no business confiding in a civilian. "I ran into Leila, his wife, at the pharmacy a couple days ago when I went in for allergy medicine."

Even with the pause, Ezra waited for me to finish. It was something I liked about him. He rarely talked over me or made big assumptions about what I was going to say next. He had so much patience. I guess having a kid at sixteen forced you to grow up quickly. Whatever made Ezra the man he was today, I was thankful.

"Shawn called because he was worried about Leila. She told him we were having lunch on Tuesday, and I think he hoped I would have some insight into her behavior. He said she's not been acting herself. Calling me about her was so stupid on his part. She's struggling with her recovery. She's in between chemo treatments, and she's not doing so good since the last one, and the doctors won't give her any more rounds until her immune system bounces back. She's probably going to need a bone marrow transplant. They're having a donor drive at the hospital for her. On top of all that, cancer freaking sucks." I didn't realize I was crying until Ezra thumbed a tear from my cheek.

"She told you all that."

"No." I sniffed. "Shawn did. Which is why the call was pointless in the first place. He knows what's going on with Leila. So, he knows better than anyone why she'd be having mood swings or personality changes. My mom was a kind woman, generous to a fault, but during the rough times, she would sometimes lash out at me. I didn't take it personally, because I knew it was more about her feelings of helplessness. The total lack of control that happens when cancer takes over your world. Hell, I lashed out at times at Gilly. Thank heavens she loved me enough to not take it to heart." I patted my cheeks. They were hot with emotion. "And that's the reason he called. I think he hoped I would reassure him. Give him a prediction or something. But I don't see the future. You know that."

My eyes felt puffy and my nose had started to run again.

"Do you want to come up to the house?" he asked.

"No, thanks. My purse is in the floorboard over there. Can you hand me the travel pack of tissues in it?"

"Are you sure you want me digging in your purse?"

"You afraid of getting bitten by my pet baby crocodile?"

He lifted an eyebrow. "Nope." He opened my bag and started searching around. "I am not seeing any tissue," he said. He started pulling items out. "Nasal spray, Vicks VapoRub, eye glass cleaner, some unscented hand cream, glasses, a brush..."

"I'm sorry." I laughed. "That bag is a black hole. Just give it here." I yanked on the purse a little too hard and the contents spilled between us. "Crap."

Ezra looked shocked as he helped me pick up the fallen items that had spilled to the floorboards. "You could win a scavenger hunt with what you have in there."

"Believe me, I need every single thing in there. Or at least I would the minute I didn't have it," I said as I retrieved my lip gloss from the seat crevice. "Better safe than sorry that you don't have..." I picked up a foil candy wrapper that was wadded into a ball, examined it, then tossed it in a cup holder. "Well, I probably don't need that."

"Aha!" Ezra held out the tissue pack and handed me one. "Here you go."

Something hard was under my thigh. I dug it out. It was small, rectangular, and was wrapped in masking tape. There was writing on the side, but I couldn't read it without my glasses. It had come out of my purse, though, so I'd probably picked it up at some point. I tossed it back inside and took the tissue from Ezra.

He gave me a sad smile. "So how did the topic come around to Fiona?"

I blew my nose. Sooo sexy. "I asked. When we were married, Shawn used to tell me stuff about work all the time, but I wish he'd kept this little nugget to himself. I think he's just...lost. You know?"

Ezra nodded. "Did he say why there's no record of it? It would have been big news to have Reagan McKay's daughter on trial for selling drugs."

"He said that Detective Lopez arrested her, and that she traded information on her distributor, like a confidential informant, to have the charges dropped."

He narrowed his gaze at me. "He told you all that?"

I shrugged. "He asked me to keep the information to myself. He doesn't want Reese or her family to find out."

"I'm sure he doesn't. Fiona's dad, Reagan McKay, paid a lot of money to get Aaron Trident re-elected mayor in the last election. Chief Rafferty's job is appointed by the mayor."

I stared at him. "Do you really think Shawn would cover up something so awful just to keep his job?"

"Do you? You know him better than I do," Ezra pointed out.

"Shawn always had a strict moral and ethical code, and while people do change, I can't see him changing *that* much."

Ezra nodded. "Is that all?"

"I wish," I said. "When I was leaving Players tonight, I ran into Phil Williams again. Gilly was with me. He put two and two together, and now he knows my face and my name. I'm on his radar, and it's freaking me out."

Ezra scrubbed his face. "Damn it."

"What?"

"I've been getting threats, warning me to drop the Williams case."

"You've been getting threats? Since when? Why am I just finding out now?" My mind leaped to the worst thing I could think of. "Please don't tell me he's leaving dead animals on your porch."

"No, nothing like that. Voicemails, printed notes, *You're Dead* keyed into my truck door when I was at the store the other day. I didn't tell you because, until the keying, I didn't think the threats were serious. I still don't. Not really. They're warnings. No one warns you if they're serious about killing you."

I nodded. "Maybe that's true. But I still would have liked to have known. Can you trace any of that?"

"The voicemails were left with burner phones purchased in another county. I've been in contact with the police there, but they came up with a dead end. The printed note was standard computer laser printer and paper. The forensics team says it's impossible to determine where it was printed since almost everyone in the world has a printer now. And whoever keyed my truck wore gloves. There were no fingerprints. Whoever is doing this is smart." He grimaced. "I'm not worried for me, but I have Mason with me now, and I don't want my job putting him in danger."

"I'll worry about you, then," I said. I gave his waist a meaningful glance. "And you must be a little worried because you're wearing a gun girdle."

Ezra smiled and shook his head. "I prefer the term carry-conceal corset." He took my hand. "Do you think that Fiona McKay's death was a homicide?"

"According to the coroner's report—"

He squeezed my palm. "I'm asking what you think. What is your gut telling you?"

"My gut thinks it's something more than an accident. But I can't decide whether I think someone drowned her or if she committed suicide."

"Huh. Suicide? What makes you think that?"

"There's something else I found out. Fiona was pregnant. Three months, according to her friend Chad. But Shawn didn't mention the pregnancy when he ran down the ME report to me. So, maybe she lost the baby, or lied to Chad about being pregnant. I don't know why— it wasn't like he was the one she was trying to rope in with the news."

"Anything else?" Ezra asked.

I nodded and continued. "Also, she has a scar on her

left wrist. She wore a cuff bracelet, so I didn't see it personally, but in my vision of her Narcotics Anonymous meeting, it was on display. Two inches long, and the thickness of the scar means it was probably pretty deep. No thin hesitation marks." I touched my wrist. "If she had tried before, she might do it again if she was distraught enough. I don't know. Fiona seemed like she could be pretty self-destructive. It's not a stretch to think she pulled the plug on herself."

Ezra was assessing me quietly.

"What?" I asked.

"You would have made a great cop, Nora. You have good observation skills and keen instincts. I hate to say it, but I didn't even notice the scar on her wrist. And the medical examiner didn't mention it."

"Maybe you can talk to Reese. She might know when and why the cut happened. I could be wrong. Maybe she'd snagged her wrist on barbwire or something. I just...have a feeling."

"Is there anything else?"

"No." I sighed wearily. "That's all I know. Do you want me to ask Reese about Fiona tomorrow? If she has any idea how the scars got on her cousin's wrist?"

"Reese came to you for help, so she would probably be less likely to throw up walls about it."

"Can you talk to the medical examiner?" I asked. "See if there's anything that might have given him even the tiniest pause before calling it an accident? And ask him to give her a pregnancy test."

"Sure." Ezra tapped his lower lip. "This is not an open investigation, so there shouldn't be any conflicts as far as the police are concerned. But," he said, "we should tread carefully. Fiona's father, Reagan McKay, is a big deal in Garden Cove, and he was understandably upset when I talked to him. He won't like it if we paint his daughter in a bad light."

"Are you saying you agree with Shawn? That keeping an ugly secret is a kindness for the family?"

"Maybe. I'd want to know. I think." He shook his head. "It's a thorny trail."

"Then we'll be careful." I looked up the road at Ezra's cabin, wanting nothing more than to go inside and have him hold me all night. "I should go home."

"Before you do, I wanted to ask... Do you want to see the fireworks tomorrow night with me? Mason's grandparents are picking him up and taking him to Portman's big extravaganza tomorrow night. He's planning on staying the night. We could have some alone time with a picnic down on the dock, making love under the fireworks."

"While you give me fireworks," I added.

He kissed me. "Exactly."

"So where is this dock where you plan to get me naked?"

"It's small, but it's down a trail out back of the cabin. Which you'd know about if you spent more time at my place," he added. He traced the outside of my thighs. "So, fireworks?" he asked. "Alone. Just the two of us?"

I rotated in the seat, carefully maneuvering over the middle console, and climbed onto Ezra's lap. I kissed him.

"Is that a yes?"

"Oh yeah," I said.

He grasped my legs and tugged me into a tight straddle. Which would have been sexy as hell if I my back spasm hadn't picked that exact moment to flare up. Only much, much worse than it had been before.

"Oh, gawd," I cried out in pain. A slight tickle in my nose had me turning my face to the window as an explosive sneeze took the pain to critical. I sounded like a dying cow as I let out an unintelligible noise.

"Are you okay?" Ezra asked.

Mortification threatened to choke me as I tried to hold myself ramrod stiff. "Back," I said on a pant. "It's my back."

Being fifty-one was awesome.

CHAPTER 13

"I don't need to go to the emergency room," I said, kneeling in the floorboard on the passenger side of my car. I gripped the seat, drawing in slow breaths. I'd discovered, when Ezra was crawling out from under me, that I couldn't bend at the waist without experiencing blinding agony. As it was, my current position was barely tolerable. "I need to lie down. I'll be okay if you take me home." I groaned. "This is so embarrassing."

Ezra shook his head. "There's nothing to be embarrassed about. I've had severe back spasms, Nora. You'll feel a lot better once the docs give you pain meds and a muscle relaxer."

We hit a bump, and I whimpered. "Okay."

After Ezra had gotten free of me, he'd ran back to his cabin for his wallet, and to let his son know why he was suddenly taking off in the middle of the night. I wondered how *that* conversation went. *Hoo boy*. "What did you tell Mason?"

"The truth."

I blinked at him. "The whole truth?" I'm not sure the sixteen-year-old wanted to hear about his dad's make-out session.

The corner of his mouth quirked up in a smile. "Maybe not the whole truth. I told him you injured your back and that I was taking you to the hospital."

"This is humiliating."

He reached for the radio. "Maybe some music will calm your nerves." He pushed the on button. John Cougar's "Jack and Diane" started playing mid-song. "Cool. I love the classics," Ezra said.

I stared at him as he pounded out the drumbeats on my steering wheel.

He glanced at me. "What?"

This was the music I'd grown up with. This was Cougar before he was Cougar Mellencamp, and Ezra calling it classic made me feel ancient. "Really? You know this song came out when I was a freshman in high school, right?"

He snickered, and I could see he was holding back a full-on laugh. After he took a few seconds to regain control, he said, "I told you, sweetheart. I love the classics."

My pulse quickened. Did he just profess his love and call me old all in the same breath? Was I happy or horrified? Most certainly both. I softened my expression then then reached back to turn the dial up as Cougar hit the chorus.

Two more "classic" songs later, and Ezra was pulling into the emergency room roundabout. He stopped in front of the doors, put the car in park, got out, and ran inside. A few minutes later, he returned with a wheelchair and a large middle-aged man with shaggy salt-and-pepper hair and a burly beard.

"Nora, this is Bear," Ezra said. "He's going to help get you inside."

I nodded. "Thanks, Bear."

"Nora, can you lift yourself up and swing your legs out of the car?" Bear asked.

I tried, but I'd spent nearly half an hour in this position, and everything below my knees had fallen asleep. "I'm afraid not. I can't move my legs."

"From your back injury?" Bear's voice sounded worried.

"Poor circulation," I said. Now, my mortification was complete. "It happens."

"That happens to me if I sit on the toilet too long," Bear offered in solidarity.

"Good to know," I said as I glanced at Ezra. He was fighting a smile again. "I think you guys are going to have to lift me out." I turned slightly to give them my arms and cried out as my back seized up. "Flippity flippin' flipping shit!"

"You okay?" Ezra asked.

"Do I sound okay?" I choked out. "Sorry, sorry." It wasn't his fault I was in this predicament. Not completely. Still, I glared at him. Another twinge caught me off guard. I grimaced. "Yeah. It's fine. I'm peachy." I looked at the wheelchair. "Even if you get me out of this car, there's no way I can sit in that," I said. "Sitting on anything isn't an option."

"Don't worry, Nora," Bear said. "I've got you." He retrieved a large dinosaur of a phone from his pocket and pressed a button before putting it to his ear. After a few seconds, he said, "I'm in the ambulance bay with a —" He covered the phone and asked, "How old are you?"

I groaned, but this time it wasn't only because of the back pain. "I'm fifty-one, damn it."

"I'm here with a fifty-one-year-old woman—" He covered the phone again. "How tall are you?"

"Next you'll be wanting my weight," I gritted out.

"Actually..."

I growled at Bear, and if my stupid legs had been working, I would have lunged for his throat.

"Dude," Ezra said with a warning headshake.

Bear, who outweighed me by at least a hundred pounds, blanched. He took his hand away from the phone receiver. "Just bring a gurney," he said, "STAT."

A young man brought out the gurney, and after an excruciating transfer, Bear and Ezra got me onto the rolling bed and took me inside. The waiting room had a dozen or more people, one guy with two tampons shoved up his bloody nose as a woman pressed ice to his face, and another guy holding his arm in an unnatural position. We passed through automatic doors, the gurney hit some kind of threshold bump, and I bit my tongue to keep from screaming.

"She needs something for pain," Ezra demanded. "Now!"

A female nurse with kind eyes and a bouncy blonde ponytail opened the door to a treatment room with the number six on the door. As Bear wheeled me in, I saw Jordy Hines standing outside a treatment room a couple of doors down. Our eyes met briefly, but the pain was too intense for me to even say hi.

The nurse took my blood pressure and temperature. She and Bear transferred me to the hospital bed. It hurt nearly as bad as the transfer from the car to the gurney.

"Ezra," I said. Tears leaked from my eyes.

"I'm here." He grabbed my hand and scowled at Bear. "Doctor," he ordered. "Now."

"Take it easy, Easy," the burly man said. "I'll go see if he's available."

"I'm a mess," I moaned.

His brow pinched with worry as he used his free hand to brush back my hair. "Everyone has stuff, Nora."

"Yeah, but I can't even make out with my boyfriend in a car without it becoming a medical emergency. That's not normal stuff."

The lines around his eyes softened. "Your boyfriend, huh?"

"You know what I mean." The spasm gripped me again, and I groaned as I moved up off my hip then lay back flat when the agony intensified more. "That's worse," I panted.

"The doctor will be in here soon." He kissed me.

The first time he'd kissed me—and I mean, good and kissed me—was in the emergency room. "We have to stop coming to this place," I told him.

The sharp scent of hand gel and medicinal antiseptic permeated the room.

A man bangs his hand against a pale-yellow wall. I recog-

nize it as the emergency ward at the Garden Cove Hospital. I also recognize the man. It's Ezra. He's wearing hospital scrubs that are too small for his boxer's build, and the short sleeves fit snug against his biceps.

A woman in uniform—who I'm sure is Reese McKay, by the color of her hair—stops in front of him. "They've stabilized Grigsby."

"Dirty bastard." Ezra puts his forearm against the wall and leans into it. "So, he's going to live, eh?"

"Looks like," Reese says. "What about Nora? Did the bullet hit anything major?"

Ezra shakes his head. "Doctor says she's going to be fine. He's cleaning the wound now so he can stitch her up." He glances to the left.

"You can't blame yourself, Easy. Nora asked to help, and she would have put her nose into this investigation whether you wanted it there or not. You can't beat yourself up about it."

He doesn't look back at Reese, he keeps his head turned to the left, presumably toward the rooms. "I know. Go on home, Reese."

"You want me to stay?" Hesitantly, she touches his arm.

He turns his head now and looks down. "Go home, Officer McKay."

"Oohhh," I grinded out as another sharp twist of the spasm knife welcomed me back from the memory.

"Where'd you go?" Ezra asked.

I'd seen a few memories of his, but he didn't have a lot of strong emotional connections to scents, so none of them had been too private. But watching the interaction between him and Reese had made me feel yucky. "Did you and Reese ever date?"

"No," Ezra said. "I've never dated Reese McKay." He frowned. "Why? What did you see?"

"The night I was shot in the leg and the doctor made you wait outside the room."

Ezra chuckled at the memory. "I was ready to kick his ass."

"Reese acted like there might have been something..."

"There wasn't," he assured me. "I'd never date a subordinate. As the saying goes, you don't crap where you eat."

I was relieved.

There was a knock, and the door opened. "Hello, Ms. Black. I see we meet again, and no bullet wound this time, right?"

"Dr. Allen," Ezra said. "Nora's having an intense back spasm. You need to do something."

"I'm not above kicking you out of the room again, Detective."

"I'm not here as a detective," Ezra said.

"Oh." Dr. Allen raised his bushy brows and peered at Ezra over his reading glasses. "Then what?"

"I'm her..." He glanced at me. "I'm her boyfriend, and I'm not leaving her alone again."

Dr. Allen sighed. "Ms. Black, when did the spasm start."

"Two days ago," I said. "The first time was at work."

"Which side?"

"Left."

The doctor walked to the left side of the bed. "Can you roll to the right for me?"

With Ezra's help and a lot of teeth gritting, I managed to get on my side. "It's just to the left of my spine above my hip. That's where the pain is the worst."

"Were you picking up something heavy?"

I winced as he poked around. "Does it matter?"

"It might."

I sighed then admitted, "I sneezed."

The doctor stopped poking the area. "You what?"

"I sneezed," I repeated. I avoided eye contact with Ezra, I didn't want to see how horrified he was that his old girlfriend threw her back out because of allergies. "Pollen is up."

"Uh-huh," the doctor said. "You'd be surprised at the amount of sneeze injuries I see in the spring."

"Really?"

The doctor nodded. "Chest and back injuries." He began pushing around again. "Usually in older patients." My death glare caused him to add, "But not always."

"Ow," I said to both his probing and his words. "That hurts."

"Are you allergic to any medications, Ms. Black?"

"Nope. Not that I know of."

"What medications are you currently on?"

"Claritin, Pseudo-Act, Ibuprofen, and Estradiol patches."

"For menopause?"

Dr. Allen was killing me. It wasn't like Ezra didn't know I'd had a hysterectomy but did the freaking doctor have to keep reminding both of us of my age?

"Yes," I said. "Surgical menopause. I had a hysterectomy in January."

"Uh." He pulled a small tablet from his lab coat and began tapping on the screen. "The nurse will come in with a shot of morphine and a shot of Depo-Medrol to help with pain and inflammation. What pharmacy do you use?"

"Craymore's," I said. "Isn't morphine extreme?"

"Your back is seized up, and that spasm is not letting go. It works quickly and will last for four to six hours, so you can get home to bed and on your way to recovering."

I'd had morphine after my hysterectomy and I didn't remember any lingering side effects, so I said, "Fine. Anything to get rid of this pain."

Dr. Allen nodded. "I'll send over a script for a muscle relaxer and some tramadol to help you through the next couple of days. You'll need to take it easy, drink plenty of water...dehydration can make spasms worse. And the medication can make you really drowsy; you'll want to have someone stay with you tonight."

"She can come home with me," Ezra said.

I hurt too much to argue.

Dr. Allen nodded. "Take care of yourself, Ms. Black."

When he left the room, I said, "I don't like that man. Not one single bit."

"His bedside manner sucks," Ezra agreed.

"Are you sorry?" I asked.

"For what?"

"For getting involved with me."

The worry lines in his forehead eased. "No way." He

rubbed my upper arm. "Are you okay coming home with me? I would go to your place, but Mason..."

"Oh, yeah. How is that going to work? Mason might not like me invading his space." Besides, the idea of Ezra taking care of me while I was laid up made my stomach and chest hurt. Old and infirmed was not how I wanted him to see me.

"He won't care."

"I think you underestimate a teenager's capacity for caring. I can stay with Gilly. She has a fold-out couch I can sleep on."

"If that's what you want." He sounded disappointed.

"It's not what I want."

"Then come home with me."

I nodded. The nurse came in shortly with two big shots, both in my backside, substantially lower than the spasm. She told me to give it fifteen minutes or so to work. Shortly after she left the room, the relief kicked in and I felt woozy. I sighed and gave my back a gentle stretch.

Shouting out in the hall harshened my newfound Zen. "What is going on out there?"

Ezra sprinted across the room and opened the door. "Shit."

"What is it?" I tried to get up but I felt loosey-goosey.

"There's a fight going on. Be right back." Then he was gone, the door shutting behind him.

CHAPTER 14

*S*ome of the loose left the goose, and I eased up to a sitting position. Crap on a cracker. My back still hurt, but not with the same intensity. I stood up, waited a couple of seconds for the dizziness to pass and staggered to the open door. Opening it was a lot harder than it should've been, but I finally managed it.

I heard Jordy shout, "Hey, back off."

Uh-oh. I peeked around the corner. Jordy was holding back the guy I'd seen with tampons sticking out his nose. Ezra was running interference with the broken arm guy. What the heck was going on?

"Hey," I called out. "Stop it. Sshtop fighting." Gosh, I felt tired. And floaty. I took a step out of the room, and without the doorjamb to support me, I stumbled to my knees.

"Nora!" Ezra said. He and Jordy, along with Bear, raced to me.

"At least my little trip stopped the yelling," I said. Then giggled. "Trip. Trip-puh. Trippy."

"I think someone's tripping, all right," Ezra said as he lifted me up into his arms.

"Is she high?" Jordy asked.

I leaned my head back, reached over and booped Jordy's nose. "Takes one to know one," I said.

Ezra smiled at me. "They gave her morphine for her back," he said.

"I think it's working."

"Lord almighty, Nora," I heard Pippa squawk.

I whipped my head toward her voice. "Pippaaaa." Right behind her was Gilly. "And Gilly-billy. My two bestie bosom buddies in the whole wide world."

"What's wrong with her?" Gilly demanded.

Ezra carried me back into the room and gently put me on the bed. "She's fine. Her back spasmed—"

"Again?" Gilly asked. "Dang, Nora. I told you to take it easy."

"Don't blame Ezra," I said. "It's not his fault I'm falling apart."

Gilly shook her head. "I'm not blaming him, dodo. I'm blaming you. You need to start taking better care of yourself."

"Yes, Mom." So damn sleepy. I was numb, and for once, it was a nice numb. I pointed at Jordy. "Hey."

"Hey," he said. "I called Pippa when I saw you come in."

That's how they knew I was here. I smiled at him. "You're okay." I twirled my finger at him. "Even if you want to get high."

His eyes bugged at me. Pippa immediately moved in

next to Jordy and took his hand. She gave him an almost imperceptible nod.

In that moment, even dosed up on drugs, I could tell that I didn't need to tell Pippa about Jordy's past. She already knew. "I guess you *can* keep secrets," I told her.

"When can Nora go home?" Gilly asked.

"The doctor says she has to be watched tonight," Ezra answered.

"Fine. I'll call the kids and have them set up the bed downstairs."

"She's coming back to my place," Ezra said. "I can handle whatever she needs."

I giggled. "Yeah, you can. Booty call," I hooted. "Booty. Booo-tee. Booty. Booo—" The word was fun to say. I pinched my cheeks. "Woowoo."

"Are you sure?" Gilly wrinkled her nose. "She's pretty out of it. And I know Nora. She can be a handful when she's recuperating."

"Look, Gilly. Nora told me what good care you took of her after her surgery, and I know you'd do a great job being there for her tonight but...I love her. And while I don't want to get between the two of you, I do want a chance to show her that I can be there for her too."

You could have heard a pin drop.

From the door, Bear said, "Damn, Easy, that was beautiful."

"I concur," I said. "And I slur," I added on another giggle.

"Then it's settled." Gilly came around and knelt by the bed. "You're going home with Ezra tonight."

She was close enough for me to boop her nose, so I did. "Don't you mean Detective Hottie?"

* * *

I WOKE up at four a.m., according to the digital alarm clock sitting in front of my face. It was not mine. I rolled onto my back, my body stiff from hard sleep. I stretched to test my back, and it was still sore, but it was no longer screaming at me.

I glanced around the room. Not mine either. I tried to piece together what had happened at the hospital after the nurse had given me the shots. All of it was mostly fuzzy. Jordy was in a fight. I remember Gilly and Pippa showing up. I also remembered acting like a complete ass. I'd have to apologize to Jordy. I hadn't meant to out him in front of a roomful of people.

A soft snore drew my attention. I rolled onto my left side to face Ezra, who was asleep on his back next to me. He had one arm over his head and one across his stomach.

I put my hand on his chest and played with the smattering of hair he had between his pecs. He didn't open his eyes right away, but his lips curled into a smile.

"Good morning," I said.

He turned his head, opened his eyes, and met my gaze. "Don't you mean, good morning, Detective Hottie?"

"Whaaat?" I said slowly and with no surprise at all. "I guess I said that, didn't I?"

"You did." He pressed his palm against my cheek.

"Are you feeling better? Do you want a pain pill or muscle relaxer? Bear gave me some samples of what the doctor prescribed you to tide you over until I can get to the pharmacy."

"I'm okay right this minute." I didn't enjoy feeling loopy, and the pain wasn't bad enough to go there again. "Thanks for taking care of me."

"I want to, Nora. I meant what I said to Gilly."

"What did you say to—" I remembered now. "Oh."

"I love you, Nora." He smiled again. "It's okay if you don't want to say it back. It's even okay if you don't feel the same way. But I don't want there to be any mistaking how I feel. You will never have to guess about me. I'm all in with you."

My heart was in my throat. I'd been in love a couple of times in my life, but none with the same fire that I'd loved Shawn, so I had given up on finding anyone for a lasting relationship. Then Ezra came along. "I love you, too. I think you know that. If you didn't, I'm saying it now. I won't promise you forever, because I don't want you to ever feel like you have to stay with me. But I can promise to love you as long as you want me."

"And if that's forever?"

"Then I'll count myself lucky." I wasn't sure he'd feel the same a year from now, but I wasn't going to spoil what we had by worrying over it.

"I did call the M.E.'s office after I got you to bed last night. It turns out that Fiona *was* pregnant. And the scar on her wrist was a self-inflicted wound from when she was seventeen."

"I think I need to speak to her parents," I said. "Do

you think they would talk with me?"

"Reese could probably arrange something informal. I called her, too, and caught her up."

"Everything?"

"I left out the drug charge and the pregnancy. That's not something you tell over the phone."

"Fair enough," I said. I glanced over at the clock. It was three minutes after four now. "How long have I been asleep?"

"Four hours. We got back here around midnight, but you fell asleep on the way home."

I groaned.

"Are you having more pain?"

"No. The shop is going to be packed. I can't leave Pippa and Gilly to work it alone."

"You want to try and work? After last night?"

"I'm feeling much better now." I patted his chest. "Thanks to you. I'll stay for another hour or so, but then I'm going to have to go home and get ready for work."

"You're crazy. And the doctor said you had to rest."

"I'm fine. Really. Classic Nora," I said, referring back to when he said he loved the classics. "I've always been a workaholic."

"I won't tell you not to go, because you can make your own decisions, but I will say that I enjoyed having you in my bed."

"Then we'll have to do it again." I scooted over and put my head in the crook of his shoulder. "What did Mason say?"

"Not a lot. He asked if you were okay."

"He's not mad I'm here?"

"Nah. I think he was impressed with the quick way you acted at the restaurant when you found Fiona. By the way, what were you doing under the dock?"

I chuckled, my breath ruffling the hairs on his chest.

Ezra squirmed. "That tickles."

"I only found her because I was trying to stretch out these stupid muscles in my back. I'd wanted to find a place secluded enough to do it without an audience."

"That makes so much more sense. I thought maybe the bathroom was full, since the women's bathrooms sometimes have a line, so you went outside to find a place to pee."

I laughed hard enough that I thought I might spasm again. "You thought I'd gone under the dock to pop a squat?"

"It crossed my mind."

"I haven't gone to the bathroom in an outdoor space since college, and only once then because I was at a house party, and some dick had stuffed the toilets with socks, and I really had to go."

"Socks?"

"Yeah, like twenty pair. The two bathrooms were completely flooded."

He pulled me in close and kissed me.

"Yuck," I said. "I haven't brushed my teeth."

"I have extra toothbrushes in the top left drawer, along with travel-sized toothpaste."

"Ready for company, huh?"

"It's what they send home with me from my dental checkups." He reached around and squeezed my butt.

159

"You brush your teeth, I'll brush mine, and then we'll figure out a few ways to pass that hour before you need to go home."

I giggled. "And here I thought I was going to have to wait until tonight for fireworks."

* * *

I DROVE HOME FEELING MORE relaxed than I had in weeks. Ezra was better than any Flexeril pill the doctor could prescribe. As I pulled up into my drive, I was sure there wasn't anything that could spoil my excellent mood.

I was wrong.

The first thing I noticed was the big black X across my door in what I guessed was spray paint. My living room window was broken, with a big, jagged, gaping hole in the glass on the right side, and my row of potted poppies had been smashed to bits.

I backed out and drove until I couldn't see my house. I pulled off to the side of the road, shaking like crazy as I searched for my phone. I called Ezra.

"Hey, sexy," he said. "Missing me already?"

"Ezra," I said, my voice trembling.

His tone sobered. "What's wrong? Are you in pain again? Do you want me to come get you?"

"My house," I said. "Someone broke into my house."

"Are they still there?"

"I don't know. I didn't stick around to find out."

"Smart." I heard him opening and closing drawers. "You call 9-1-1. I'm on my way."

CHAPTER 15

*N*ausea and fear roiled inside me as I waited for Ezra, Jeanna Treece and her partner, Levi Walters, to clear my house. The intruder, whoever he or she was, had thrown one of my flowerpots through the living room window. The downside of living without neighbors was that it had given the burglar free rein to trash my place.

I rubbed my arms. What if I'd been home? The thought chilled me to the bone. What would I have done if I'd been here alone? I had a gun, and I'm sure I would have used it. After all, I had a strong sense of self-preservation. Just ask Carl Grigsby.

Ezra stepped outside. His lips thinned as rage simmered in his narrowed gaze. "It's pretty bad in there, but it's okay to come in now."

Officer Treece, who had cut her brown hair short recently, stood inside by my broken television and was taking a picture of the mess in my living room.

"I'm so sorry this happened, Ms. Black," she said.

"The thief did a pretty thorough job of trashing the place."

I shook my head and thanked God I had good home owner's insurance. "A thief would have stolen the television, not vandalize it."

She nodded. "Still, you need to look around and see if anything's missing."

Levi Walters, a thin, young officer with jet-black hair and dark brown eyes, bounded down my staircase. "The bedroom is a mess. The bed has been sliced up, the curtains shredded. The perpetrator even tossed your drawers and yanked all the clothes out of your closet."

Ezra put his arm around me. "Except for some of the more straightforward destruction, it seems like someone was searching for something."

"But what?" I glanced at Ezra. "My gun. I keep it in the nightstand in a locked case."

"I didn't see a gun case," Levi said.

"Maybe it was teenagers," Jeanna said. "It's Memorial weekend, and bad decisions are running rampant with the youth. I arrested two boys last night who got drunk and tried to knock each other out."

I shook my head, but said, "Maybe."

I went upstairs, my spirit crushed by what had been done to my home. Ezra followed. I was grateful for his company as I walked the short distance to my bedroom.

"Fu-udge," I said on a hard exhale. "He destroyed everything. Damn it." Angry tears burned my eyes. It looked like Wolverine had used his adamantium claws to slice and dice my mattress. Not an easy task, considering it was a high-end memory foam mattress. My feather pillows were mutilated, and my clothes scattered on the floor. This was malicious. "Why would someone do this? I don't get it."

"Do you think anyone knows you're looking into Fiona's death?"

"Why would that matter? There's nothing in this house that relates to Fiona or her drowning." I shook my head. "This feels angry and personal. I don't know anyone who hates me this much."

My thoughts went to Phil Williams. He had to know I was the one who'd taken down his lackey cop. And maybe Gio? Nah. He might be a class-A douchenozzle, but I didn't believe he would do this. It had to be Phil, right? "You think Williams has been sending you threats? Do you think this was his doing as well? Would he come after me like this?"

"I don't know. God, I hope not."

I picked up a pillow with feathers poking out of a gaping wound. My lower lip jutted in a pout. "I loved that bed."

He put his arms around me, the ripped-up pillow smooshed between us, and held me tight. "I loved it, too."

A faint scent wafted up from the pillow. "What is that?"

Ezra let me go. "What? Do you see something?"

More like smell something. I put the pillow to my nose and inhaled. "Peppermint. A hint of tea tree." I sniffed again. "Son-of-a-bitch."

"Are you getting one of your visions?"

"Nope," I said. "But I don't need one. I know who did this."

"How? I mean, if you didn't see anything."

"Because the bastard that did this has been in my shop several times this month. And yesterday, he bought my argan shampoo and coconut conditioner for men. I smell peppermint, tea tree, and coconut on this pillow. It *has* to be him."

"Do you know his name?"

"No, but I can describe him. Tall, dark hair, graying sideburns, and he's allergic to apple pectin."

"That's oddly specific," Ezra said.

"He asked me if there was any in the shampoo. Do you think he's been stalking me? His sideburns reminded me of a country singer my father loved."

"Merle Haggard?"

"Yes!"

Ezra gave me a half smile. "Do you think you might have a receipt with his name on it or something?"

"Pippa rang him up. She'll know." I looked for my alarm clock. It was on the floor next to my empty dresser, and it looked like someone had tried to stomp a hole into it. "Do you know what time it is?"

Ezra looked at his watch. "Eleven-forty," he said.

I had a surge of panic. "I need to call Pippa. I'm surprised she isn't blowing up my phone."

"She was at the hospital last night, remember? She probably thinks you're still in bed."

I scoffed. "She knows me better than that." I reached over to grab my phone out of my purse and realized I didn't have it. "I left my bag in the car."

"You can use my phone if you want."

"Unless you have Pippa's number in your contact list, it's not going to do me any good."

He nodded toward the door. "Let's go get your phone."

Every step that I took in my house, my chest hurt. The place I'd loved yesterday had become something monstrous to me. It enraged me that Sideburns Guy had taken away my sense of safety in my own home. As I exited the front door, I blew out a breath I didn't even realize I'd been holding.

"Slow down, Nora," Ezra said. "You don't want to tweak your back again."

"I've got to get away from that." I jerked my thumb over my shoulder without looking back at the house. I stumbled to the side of the drive and threw up near one of the shattered poppies.

Ezra's hand was on my back, holding my hair away from my face. Gilly would have been proud of him for the doing just the right thing. "Are you okay? Maybe we should go back to the ER."

I shook my head, my throat burning as I wretched again. A combination of nerves and medication. The nurse had warned me that stomach upset was a potential side effect.

"I'm okay," I managed on a wheeze. I stood up and wiped my mouth with the back of my hand. "I feel better."

"You sure?"

I took a steadying breath. "Yes." The nausea was

gone. "It's passed. You happen to have any gum on you?" I asked.

"It just so happens I do," he replied with a smile, handing me a piece.

"You might be perfect," I teased, popping the gum into my mouth gratefully.

"I try," Ezra said with a chuckle.

I went to the car and got into the driver's seat. Ezra went around the other side, and joined me. He handed me my purse from the floor.

"Here you go." He pinched the bridge of his nose.

"Headache?"

"Uh-huh," he said. "It's been a long two days."

"I got you," I began plucking through my purse, "I have some ibuprofen in here somewhere." I pulled out the tissues, the Vicks, a hairbrush, and the small taped rectangle. I handed it to Ezra. "Can you tell me what this is?" I dug out my glasses next and put them on. I should have done that first, because I could finally see well enough to find the bottle of pain reliever. "Ah ha! Found them." My mouth was still sour, so when I spied some mints, I grabbed those as well.

"Nora?" Ezra said.

"What?" I glanced over at him. He was holding up the taped object. I pushed my glasses up my nose and peered closer. "Is that a USB drive?"

"It is."

"Does that say F. McKay on the tape?"

Ezra nodded. "It certainly does."

"How in the world did that get in my purse?"

I flashed back to the pharmacy when Fiona had

stumbled into me. Had it been a ploy to drop the drive into my purse? Had Phil Williams' arrival prompted her to hide it?

"I think Fiona might have dropped this in my purse at the pharmacy. But why?"

Ezra's shrewd gaze narrowed on the drive. "I guess we should get to a computer and find out."

"I don't want to go back in the house to see if my laptop survived. We can use the computer at Scents and Scentsability."

* * *

"Oh my gosh, Nora. What are you doing here? You should be home in bed," Pippa railed at me when I arrived. "And shame on you, Easy, for not giving her a *reason* to stay in bed."

"It's not Ezra's fault," I said in my guy's defense. "I knew today would be busy. You shouldn't have to handle it all by yourself."

"And I'm not. Gilly's in the back with a client right now, but she's been on the floor with me a lot today helping with customers."

The shelves were half empty. "It looks like business has been good."

"It's been completely manic since we opened. We've had a hundred customers in today, and I'm exhausted," Pippa said. "I'm not one to complain about good business but thank heavens there's only one more day of this coming. I'm not sure we have enough stock to last," she added. She waved at Ezra. "Sorry I yelled at you."

"I've got broad shoulders," Ezra said.

Then she turned back to me. "I'm not sorry I yelled at *you*, though. You should be home. You really scared me last night. When Jordy called, I thought you were dying."

"I'm sorry. I didn't mean to worry you." I wasn't ready to talk about the ransacking of my house, yet.

"Not your fault." She kissed my cheek. "I forgive you. You can make it up to me by seeing if you can pull some soap molds early."

"Of course. I'm sure I have a dozen batches."

I scanned the half-empty shelves. "And I'll grab some lotions and oils as well."

Pippa pointed to the shampoo and conditioner display. "Do you have any of that shampoo left? The men's dandruff shampoo with argan and tea tree?"

"We're out? I had a dozen bottles up there yesterday."

"The man who'd come in the day before returned bright and early to purchase our entire shelf of stock." She smiled triumphantly. "I guess he really liked them."

"Wait? What? He came back here this morning?"

Ezra had caught what Pippa said as well. "What time was he here?"

"I don't know..." Pippa's nostrils flared. "Is something wrong?"

"Try to remember," I said. "It's important."

"Maybe nine-ish." She shrugged. "What's the big deal? Please don't tell me there's something wrong with the shampoo."

"Did he leave his name?" Ezra asked.

I gripped her arm, but not hard.

"Ow," she said. She was wearing long sleeves, and I remembered the road rash.

"I'm sorry. We really need to know. Did the man leave his name or contact information?"

"No." Pippa shook her head. "He paid cash."

"Damn it," I hissed.

"Okay. You're starting to freak me out, Nora. What is going on? And don't mince words. Shoot it to me straight."

I gritted my teeth as my frustration reached a boiling point. "Well, Pippa, it looks like the guy who ransacked my house and vandalized it from top to bottom has become one of our best customers."

CHAPTER 16

"*D*id you say ransacked and vandalized?" Pippa's face drained of color. "Holy shite on buttermilk biscuits." Pippa hugged herself, her shoulders rounding forward, and her eyes stark with disbelief.

Ezra got on his phone. "Hey, this is Detective Holden, special crimes. Can we get a team down to Scents and Scentsability on Main Street to lift some fingerprints?" Ezra strode to the door and flipped the hanging sign to closed. "Thanks," he said into the phone. "I'll be here when you arrive."

"Tell me what happened," Pippa said.

"I got home this morning, and someone had spray-painted my door, broke my flower pots, threw one through the living room window, then, presumably, crawled inside my house and proceeded to shred and smash everything they could get their hands on."

"And...the shampoo guy did it?"

"I believe so. I'm ninety-seven percent certain it was him. I smelled a combination of the shampoo and conditioner he bought yesterday. And you know how he's been coming in and out of the shop." I clucked my tongue. "I think he was stalking me."

"Whatever for?"

"Honestly, I don't know." The man had started coming into the shop before I'd even met Fiona, so it couldn't have been about her. "I have to assume it has something to do with my involvement in the Lloyd Briscoll case, but I have no idea if that's it or not."

"This is some next-level nasty," Pippa said. "I never thought—" She shook her head. "I haven't been to my house in a couple of days. What if..."

The fact that she hadn't been home didn't escape me. It reminded me that we still needed to have a chat about Jordy. I wasn't sure if I'd gauged her reaction correctly when I'd been wacked out on morphine. Not to mention, we'd never addressed the road rash on her arm. "It's scary bad," I agreed.

"Cripes, Nora, this surpasses scary right into the terrifying range of bad."

"I'm shook. Right to my core." I shivered, and Ezra put his arm around me again.

"Oh my gosh, Nora, what if you had been home? Thank fate and all her ugly sisters that you injured your back and stayed with Ezra."

"I'm not quite ready to feel grateful for that spasm." The extreme pain was still fresh in my memory, not to mention the slight soreness in my back. "But I am thankful I wasn't home."

She crossed her arms over her chest. "So, what are

you doing here? You should go back to Easy's and get some rest. Let the police do their job."

"I plan to." I pointed toward the workroom. "But first, we need to use the business computer."

Ezra got off the phone. "There's a team on the way. Can you let them in when they get here, Pippa? Just holler at us when they arrive." On that note, he ushered me past my worried friend and through the door into the workroom.

Ezra and I made a beeline to the desk.

I gestured for Ezra to sit in the chair, then depressed the power button on the tower situated on the left side of the desktop. "It takes a second to wake up," I said in way of explanation. "But it's not that old, so unless the drive is encrypted, you shouldn't have any problem opening it on here."

"You know about encryption?" Ezra's gaze was curious. "You don't seem like someone who pays attention to technology."

"You mean because I didn't know what an eggplant and taco in a sext meant?"

He shook his head and chuckled. "Something like that."

I put my glasses on. "The drive thingy is just under this flap." I flipped a small plastic panel open on the computer tower. "Here."

Pippa walked into the workroom. "Easy, the team you ordered is here."

Ezra glanced up at the three male officers standing with Pippa. "Can you show them the shelf where the shampoo was and anything else you remember him touching?" he asked Pippa.

"On it," Pippa replied, ushering the men back out into the shop.

"Something's happening," I muttered, watching the screen.

"It says one of ten updates are processing," Ezra said. "It's going to take a couple minutes to load."

While Ezra waited for the computer to do its thing, Pippa came back to the office and I took her aside.

"I showed them all the areas he might have touched," she said with a small shiver.

"Excellent," Ezra said, still focused on the screen.

"Thank you." I gently touched the sleeve of her shirt. I had a few minutes, and I was going to use them wisely. "How was the riding lesson the other day?" I asked.

"It was fun," she said with a shrug. She hesitated, then said, "Jordy says I'm a natural."

I arched my brow. "Is that before or after you got that road rash on your forearm? I told you we were going to talk about it. Especially since you promised me you wouldn't ride without a helmet or pads."

She puffed up her cheeks then let out the breath. "The rash happened before I could even get on the road with the bike," she admitted with a fair amount of chagrin. "Jordy was teaching me how to get the dang thing started, and I thought I had it down. So I jumped the gun, punched my foot down on the kickstart, or at least I tried to. The bottom of my boot was slick and I slipped off the lever, lost my balance, and tumbled to the ground. And to top off my humiliation, I pulled the stupid motorcycle on top of me."

"Cripes, Pippa," I squeaked. "Those things weigh like four hundred pounds. Are you okay?"

"Obviously," she said with a grin. "You see me here, walking, talking, no casts or crutches."

"Okay, smart aleck. Then what happened?"

"Jordy cleaned my arm and doctored it with antiseptic and ointment. He said it would heal faster uncovered, so I didn't put a bandage over it once it stopped bleeding."

"How did the rest of the lesson go?"

Pippa blushed and busied herself by straightening the bottom of her blouse. "Fine."

I eyed her suspiciously. "How far into the lesson did you get?"

"Honestly, we never made it back out of his house. One thing led to another, which led to another, and that all led us right into the bedroom."

I laughed. "So, when you said you were learning to ride, you weren't talking about motorcycles."

"Nora!" she said with a scandalized tone.

"Things are going good with you two."

She brushed her hair away from her face, her smile beaming. "It's wonderful. He's wonderful. He makes me feel like I'm the only woman in the world."

"I'm really happy for you, Pippa. Has he told you anything about his past?"

She stopped and looked at me. "He's not an ex-DEA agent, if that's what you're asking."

Before Pippa and Jordy began dating, she used to

muse about the history of the biker barista, and under-cover narcotics officer had been one of the many hats she'd imagined him wearing. Unfortunately, I was more worried about him being on the wrong side of the law where drugs were concerned.

"That's not what I'm asking. He's not from Garden Cove, and I was just wondering what he was doing before he decided to move to town and open a coffee shop."

She shrugged. "He worked construction in Minnesota for a while. When his grandmother died, she left him some money. He used it to move here and start a new life."

"Is that all?" When I'd been stoned on morphine and accused Jordy of loving a good high, maybe I'd imagined Pippa's knowledge of his situation. Was I sticking my nose, pun intended, where it didn't belong?

"What more do you need to know?" Her question was slightly accusing.

"I might have...seen something."

"You mean one of your..." She twirled a finger around her face. "Will it change the way I feel about Jordy?"

"Maybe."

"Then I don't want to know, Nora."

"Are you sure?"

"He's not cheating on me, right?"

"Not that I know of."

Pippa looked relieved. "Well, then I don't care what you know about him. He's a good man now, and that's all that matters."

"Okay." I nodded. "I'll respect your wishes."

"Wait." She glanced toward the front of the shop. "Does Gilly know?"

"No. I didn't tell her."

"Well, I think I know what it is, but go ahead and say it." Pippa braced herself for the incoming blow.

As gently as I could, I said, "Jordy's a recovering drug addict."

I'd expected shock and dismay. Instead, I got relief again. "He told me," she said. "Before we even went on our first date."

Now it was my turn to be relieved. "Oh. That's great, Pip. You never said."

"It's not something he's ashamed of. He even sponsors addicts. I've heard him talk more than one person on the verge of a relapse off the edge. When did you have the vision?"

"Last night at Players. One of the cooks, a guy named Chad, attends Narcotics Anonymous meetings. I saw Jordy in his memory."

Her eyes darkened and she paled. "Oh," she said.

"Do you know Chad?"

Pippa shook her head. "Last night..."

"Last night what?" I pressed.

"It's not my story to tell."

"Okay, I get that. Let's try this another way. Why was Jordy at the ER?"

She frowned. "It's called Narcotics *Anonymous* for a reason. But I will tell you that one of the guys he sponsors overdosed last night."

"Chad?" I asked, ignoring the anonymous part. I hoped not. He might have had a troubled past, but from what I knew, he seemed like a nice guy who'd fallen in a love with a girl, only to lose her. "Fiona's death was too much for him to deal with," I mused. "He really loved her."

Pippa pursed her lips. "I can't tell you who, because it's supposed to be anonymous. But I will say that his sponsee is expected to make a full recovery. However, I will also cryptically add that you are very good at guessing."

Being right didn't always feel good.

Ezra glanced up from the monitor. "Hey, you two. Updates are done and I got the drive open."

We joined him at the desk. I looked at the screen and saw one folder listed on the USB drive as DPI, and when Ezra clicked on it, it was full of spreadsheets and .docx files with undecipherable lines of numbers and letters.

"Well, crap, that's disappointing," I said.

"What were you expecting?"

"Pictures, recordings, and videos of bad guys doing bad things, of course. This might as well be gibberish."

Pippa moved closer to the monitor. "Those look like BANs."

"Say it like I'm stupid," I told her.

"Banking codes," Pippa explained. "They're identifiers for banks. I recognized that one there. GCCB20489000 is the bank identifier for Garden Cove Community Bank." She pointed at the screen. "I do most of our bills and banking online, so I'm really familiar with that one. And that line there is a routing number."

"Why would Fiona have files with bank codes and routing numbers?" I asked.

"See these columns here," Pippa directed us to two of them, "these look like money columns, and the third column is the difference between them. There are five bank codes, but I only recognize the one."

"What's going on?" Reese McKay, in uniform, joined us in the office.

I was startled to see her. "Where'd you come from?"

"I got the call to come out here and help secure the scene. I heard about your place this morning." Reese fidgeted with a lower button on her police shirt, a stricken look on her face. "Did this place get robbed, too?"

"We think the guy who dumped my house was in the shop this morning."

"I'm sorry, Nora, if this is my fault. I shouldn't have involved you in Fiona's stuff. I...I feel like I let her down when she was alive, and now I feel like I'm failing her again in death." Her voice choked.

"You need to take some time off, Reese," Ezra said. "You should be with your family."

She drew her shoulders back. "My brothers and sisters in blue are my family."

Impulsively, I hugged her. The sweet aroma of honeysuckle tickled my senses. "You smell good," I told her.

A woman stands on a boat deck. It's night. The sky is clear and bright with stars. She's wearing jeans and a light jacket. I recognize Fiona's curves, her youthful bounce, and her hair as she pushes herself off the rail and confronts a man who steps out on the deck. The smoothly sweet aroma of honeysuckle wafts through the air. "Give me the fifty thousand dollars. I'll go away, and he'll never have to see me or the baby ever."

"You shouldn't be here." *The man grabs her by the arms and gives her a shake.* "I told you to stay away from all this. You have a get out of jail free card. Use it."

Fiona yanks out of his grasp and stumbles backward. She braces herself against a metal rail. The man is wearing a hat, and in the dark, I can't make out his hair. He isn't the same guy from the first vision. He's got a different voice.

He approaches her. "Give me the files you stole, and you can be done with this."

Fiona sidesteps him. "No. It's the only leverage I have. I need to help myself. You have two weeks to get me my money, or I swear I will blow up their whole operation here in Garden Cove."

"You're bluffing."

"Try me."

I blinked as the memory left.

Ezra stood behind me. "What did you see, Nora?"

My gaze went to Reese. "Are you wearing Fiona's perfume?"

"Yes." She blushed. "It's Honeysuckle Rose. It's...it was her favorite. I took the bottle from her bedroom yesterday. Did it trigger a vision?"

"It did." And boy howdy, it had been a doozy. "I believe you, Reese. I don't think Fiona's death was an accident."

179

"*D*id you recognize anything about the man in your vision?" Ezra asked. "Or the boat?"

"No, I don't know the guy's voice. There's something familiar about him, but nothing I can nail down," I told him.

"What about hair color?" he pressed.

"He wore a hat, so it's hard to say for sure."

"Did he have sideburns?" Pippa asked.

"He had a hat on, and it was dark," I told her, shaking my head. The memory had taken place at night. The scent of honeysuckle had been less strong than the perfume. It was a cleaner scent, like the actual flower. "When did the honeysuckle start blooming around here?"

"Early May," Pippa said.

Reese nodded. "And it's all along the banks of the Cove now. Did you happen to see if the boat was in a dock or anything?"

I quirked my mouth to the side as I tried to

remember all the details. I'd assumed the boat had been in a dock, but I hadn't seen any of the overhead lights that most of the commercial resort docks had installed. Also, I gotten the impression that Fiona could get off the boat anytime she wanted to. "It had to be a private dock." I looked at Ezra. "Something like what you said you have behind the cabin. Fiona didn't look trapped. And this guy acted like he might have cared about Fiona."

Ezra scrunched his face. "So, you don't think the guy was Phil Williams?"

I'd exchanged only a few words with the man, but the encounters had left their mark on my psyche. "It wasn't him."

He narrowed his brow. "You thought Fiona had been afraid of him at the pharmacy. Do you think Phil's the man who got her pregnant?"

Reese gasped. "Pregnant?"

"I'm sorry, Reese," Ezra said, running his hand through his hair and closing his eyes for a moment. "I didn't think...I thought you knew."

Reese's stance faltered. Ezra stepped around me and helped her to a nearby stool. "I can't believe she was pregnant."

"The medical examiner put her right around three months," Ezra said.

"Fiona had always talked about being a mom when she was young. She'd obsessed over her baby dolls." Reese wrung her shaking hands together. "She had wanted to talk to me, but I wouldn't let her. When she got that DUI..." She dropped her chin down and stared at her knees. "I was so mad at her. I'd tried to help her before, but she kept messing up. Christ, I turned my back on her. What have I done? I should have been there for her."

Pippa handed Reese a tissue from a box on the computer desk. "We can't live our lives on should'ves," Pippa said. "It won't bring Fiona back, and it won't bring you any solace."

"Besides," I added. "You didn't cause Fiona's death. It was beyond your control, even if you had known. She was blackmailing the father of her baby, so she could get out of town. I don't think that would have changed even if you had known."

The sob that left Reese's throat gutted me. Her pain was raw and real. Pippa and I put our arms around her like a shield.

"I'll get to the truth of it for you. I swear it," I whispered, meaning every word.

We held her for a moment, and Ezra stayed out of the way until Reese pulled herself together. I loved that he hadn't swooped in to try and make it better. A lot of guys would have been scrambling to figure out a way to make the emotional moment stop. Sometimes people needed to cry, to let go of the pain.

"I wish I'd seen more in my vision. I think I need to see where she lived. Maybe something there might trigger my mojo." It would have been super convenient if Fiona's memory would have included some names. My frustration mounted. "Why can't I make out faces? It's just so maddening."

Reese began pacing. The rubber soles of her shoes

made a hiss sound as they scrapped along the concrete floor. "Maybe what you saw was the moments before she drowned."

"It was nighttime," I said gently. "She was wearing different clothes. Besides, I found her body around dusk, when it was still light out. The vision was later at night. I'm only guessing, but in the vision, she said the guy had two weeks to get the money. That was the same time frame she'd given Chad to decide if he wanted to go with her. So, it was probably a few weeks back."

"Chad?" Reese asked with a pained expression of confusion.

"He worked with Fiona at Players."

"You mean the cook. Big guy."

I nodded.

"I met him one time a few months ago." Reese's eyes clouded. "I didn't know they were dating."

The more we said, the more Reese realized how little she knew about her cousin. I was sure this was going to compound her guilt, but there was no time to try and soften any blows. Skirting issues to be kind could get someone killed. I had no time to die, and I wasn't going to let anyone I loved die either.

"He's a cook at Players. He loved Fiona." I recollected how she had asked Chad to come with her. "I think she might have loved him back." I grabbed Reese's hand. "Fiona had been sober for two months. No drugs. No drinking."

Even if I hadn't seen the meeting, I knew that the detective who had arrested her, Frank Lopez, had been screening her for drugs, and according to Shawn, she'd been clean every time.

"I need to talk to Chad." Reese patted her pockets as if searching for keys or a phone. "Do you have a last name?"

I glanced over at Pippa, and she nodded.

"He was in the hospital last night." I sighed. "Drug overdose. I think Fiona's death took him over the edge."

Reese closed her eyes and inhaled deeply. "Is he alive? Please tell me he's alive."

"Yes," Pippa said. "He went into a treatment program this morning."

"I want who did this to Fiona." Reese raised her chin defiantly. "I want the bastard's balls."

"And you shall have them," I said, willing it to be true. "And, if I can, I will serve them up on a platter."

"We should probably clue in the chief," Ezra said. "But I'm afraid there's still not enough to make a case. The coroner and ME had declared her drowning accidental, and it's going to take some proof for them to change their minds."

"Then let's go get some proof." I nodded to Reese. "Do you have the keys to Fiona's house?"

"I can get them," she said. "She lived in the guesthouse at my aunt and uncle's. We'll have to go over there. They'll let us in."

Ezra put the drive into his pocket. "Then we should get going."

* * *

ON A PICTURESQUE AREA of the Garden Cove Lake amidst tree-laden rolling hills, the Dogwood Hills private subdivision could only be described as palatial. The luxury estates were located three miles past the road that led to Ezra's cabin. According to Reese, four homes perched on ten acres of land, making up the entirety of Dogwood Hills.

"This wasn't here when I was in high school," I said.

"Yesterday was the first time I've ever been behind the gate of this place. The homes were built a few years back. Don and Claire Portman live over that way." Ezra pointed down an immaculately paved road that split off to the right.

The McKays' place had a private entrance with a security gate. Reese, who was in the car ahead of Ezra and me, punched the code into a panel, and we followed her inside when the gate swung open.

"It might sound naïve, but I still can't reconcile how a girl from all this privilege could've gotten herself mixed up in this mess." I stared out the window at the lush landscape marred only by a golf driving range and a tennis court. "It just goes to show you that money is no substitute for happiness."

The asphalt drive opened up to the McKay mansion, and we pulled into a turnabout where two sedans and a truck were parked. Ezra pulled in behind Reese's car.

"It looks like they already have a houseful," I said to Ezra.

"It'll take more people than what could fit in those vehicles to fill this house. Hell, half of Garden Cove could comfortably stand under the roof without bumping into a neighbor," he replied.

I'd met Reagan McKay, Fiona's dad, once when I was first looking for property for my business. He'd been eager to help me find the right location. I'd lucked out when the previous owner, Marie Tidwell sold me her place directly, allowing me to convert Tidwell's Diner into Scents & Scentsability. I hadn't seen Reagan since then.

My family hadn't been rich, but I'd always thought of my parents as affluent. I'd grown up in an upper-middle-class neighborhood. When my dad died, he'd left enough money for my mom to live comfortably for the rest of her life as long as she didn't go crazy. Unfortunately, the cancer had eaten away at her savings toward the end, and I had dipped into my own savings to pay utilities and taxes on her home. It had been my pleasure to take care of my mom.

Reese waited on the steps for us. My back had started to ache more, so I'd taken a pain pill from the sample packet. It still hadn't kicked in yet.

"You okay?" he asked.

"Terrific," I said. "Trying to stay ahead of another trip to the ER."

We got out and joined Reese.

"It looks like your aunt and uncle have guests."

"The silver car belongs to Claire Portman, Don Portman's wife." She sniffled. "She and Aunt Jenny are thick as thieves. They grew up together. I'm not sure who the others belong to, but probably a couple close friends."

"Maybe we should have called ahead."

Reese nodded solemnly. "Already did. Aunt Jenny said I could have Fiona's keys."

We followed Reese inside. She led us through a large foyer, past a central staircase, down a hall, through a giant kitchen with an industrial-sized Viking stove and oven combination. When my mom had died, my kitchen had been overwhelmed with casseroles and other dishes that could be frozen and quickly reheated. It was how communities supported their own. I glanced around at the counters and the center island. They were bare.

"What's wrong?" Ezra asked, as if sensing my unease.

"Where is all the food?" I asked quietly. "It's so...empty."

"Oh, honey, there's been plenty of food sent over." A thin woman with shoulder-length bottle-blonde hair wearing a blue blouse with peplum sleeves came into the kitchen from a hallway to the right of us. I recognized her and her misshapen lips as Lucy Campbell, the woman who'd been sitting with Big Don and his wife at Players the night before.

"I promise you," she said. "Jen's fridge and freezer are plum full." I guessed Lucy to be near my age, in her fifties, but she'd had obvious plastic surgery, so it was hard to tell.

"Hi, Lucy," Reese said. "I didn't see your car outside."

"I rode over with Jameson. He likes to drive that old truck sometimes." She gave Reese a brief hug and an air kiss on her cheek. "I don't know that I've seen you in your uniform before. You look wonderful. Your aunt Jenny is always bragging on you. How are you holding up, sweetheart?"

Reese dipped her head and looked away. "As good as I can be. I'm more worried about Aunt Jenny and Uncle Reagan. Where is everyone?"

"Reagan, Jameson, Big Don, and a few others have gathered in the smoking room." She gave Reese a wistful smile that caused a weird pucker in her upper lip. "It's good for them to be together." Lucy pivoted her gaze to Ezra and me. "Well, introduce me to your guests."

"Oh, yeah, sorry," Reese said. "This is Detective Ezra Holden and Nora Black. She's..." I could see Reese searching for a reasonable description to explain my presence.

"I'm a consultant for the Garden Cove PD," I said.

"Consultant, huh." Lucy tilted her head to the side. "Nora Black." She tapped her chin. "We used to have a chief of police named Black. Any relation?"

"He was my dad," I said.

"Connor was a decent man," she said fondly. "I guess the apple doesn't fall far from the tree."

"Easy, Nora, this is Lucy Campbell, she and her husband are part of a business group here in town with my aunt and uncle. They've all been friends for a long time."

"Nice to meet, you." I extended my hand. Lucy gave it a look then grasped just my fingertips and gave my hand a limp shake.

"The pleasure is mine," she said with a smile that didn't reach her eyes.

"Where's Aunt Jenny?" Reese asked.

"She and Claire are out by the pool." She shooed us with a quick wave of her hands. "You three go on out. I'm getting more ice for the drinks."

After we exited the kitchen through the French double doors, I spied Lucy's husband, Jameson Campbell, leaning against a pillar, his arms crossed over his chest, staring off into the distance. His hair wasn't slicked back today, and his graying locks fell against his forehead. He, like his wife, seemed more my age than the McKays and Portmans.

Reese pointed at him. "There's Jameson, Lucy's husband." She waved at him when he looked at us. He gave her a two-finger salute from his forehead then twirled his hand and gave a short bow.

Reese gave him a brief smile as we walked toward two women. Claire Portman, wife of Big Don Portman, was sitting next to a heavier set woman with dark auburn hair so much like Fiona's, it had to be her mother, Jenny McKay. The closer I got, the more I realized I had seen Jenny before. She'd come to my mom's visitation.

Her eyes were swollen and red, and there were crumpled tissues wadded up on the table. Claire was holding one of her hands, and they both had amber-colored drinks in short highball glasses, no ice.

"Wait here," Reese said. "I'll be right back." She left Ezra and me to join her aunt and Claire by the pool."

"I don't think they're drinking tea," I said.

"Probably not," Ezra agreed.

Jameson walked over to us. "It's whiskey-thirty somewhere," he said. "Hi," he held out his hand, "I'm Jameson Campbell."

"Have we met?" There was something familiar about him, but I got a lot of people coming through our shop on a daily business.

"I've seen you around, Ms. Black," he said. There was something about Jameson Campbell that churned my gut. I took a step back as the smell of honeysuckle drifted in the air.

"Come on, darlin', take a walk with me," the man says. "The lake's real pretty tonight. Not as pretty as you, of course." I recognize Jameson's slicked waves.

"You ol' so-n-so," a woman says. It's his wife, Lucy. "You always were a smooth talker."

"How else was I gonna get you to marry me?" He puts his arm around her. They walk down to the lake. Honeysuckle vines are in bloom on both sides of the trail. When they reach the dock, the man holds out his hand. He's wearing a gold ring with a black onyx stone, a half circle and line symbol cut into it.

I stared at Jameson Campbell as my vision ended. The symbol on Jameson's ring was similar if not identical to the marking I'd seen on Boot Guy's watch as he'd offered Fiona that snort of white powder. What did it mean?

"Do I have something on my face?" He touched his cheek, and I saw the ring from the memory.

So much had happened since that first Fiona vision, I couldn't tell if his voice was that of Boot's Guy, but the symbol was far too big a coincidence not to address. "Do you have a watch that matches that ring?"

He shook his head. "Not anymore. I lost it a while back," he said. "I only have the ring now. Why?"

"Does the symbol mean anything?" Ezra asked.

Jameson's smile tightened into a grimace. "It's a C, G, and an E, depending on how you look at it. Several of us got them about fifteen years ago when we started really developing tourism around here." He flushed. "It means Garden Cove Elite. Why do you want to know?"

I glanced from Jameson to Ezra. "We're going to need a list of all the men who are part of the GCE."

Jameson looked taken aback. "Why?"

Ezra put an arm around my shoulders. "Excuse us, will you?" He took me away from the frowning man. "That symbol has something do with your visions, doesn't it?"

"Yes. I saw it on Boot Guy's wristwatch." I looked over Ezra's shoulder and caught the hard stare of Jameson. "He, or one of his friends, might be the killer."

CHAPTER 18

"I can't believe anyone from our circle would have hurt Fiona," Don Portman said. "It's ridiculous. We've all watched that girl grow up. She's family."

My revelation had brought all the men outside from the house. Jenny, Claire, and Lucy were huddled together. Jenny's two friends stood on either side of her, bolstering her with support. A picture-perfect friend-ship. They reminded me of Gilly, Pippa, and myself. Always there for each other in good times and bad. But something seemed off, and I couldn't help but think that sometimes pictures were deceiving.

Ezra had asked Reagan and Big Don to join us outside. Big Don, at six foot five, towered over all of us.

"You say you got a witness who saw my girl arguing with someone wearing that watch?" Reagan McKay demanded, narrowing his eyes at me. Reagan was short and girthy with light blue eyes and a full head of silvery-gray hair. "I find it hard to believe."

We'd lied about the witness. Obviously. I didn't need more people knowing about my smell-o-vision ability.

"It's true, Uncle Reagan," Reese said.

Reagan wagged a finger at her. "No one I know would harm my child," he scoffed angrily. "The whole idea is utterly ridiculous."

"But you're willing to believe she accidentally drowned?" Jenny asked in a pained whisper.

Reagan looked at his wife, his expression full of anguish. "She..." He shook his head.

"What, Reagan?" Jenny asked. "Just tell me. I know you're holding information back. I understand you believe you're protecting me. You're not. I'm not a child, and I know Fiona had her problems. But she was getting better. She was getting back to her old self again."

"She was a drug addict," he barked. "I wanted to shield you from all this. Our daughter drowned because she was high."

Reese opened her mouth to say something, but Ezra shook his head. He clearly wanted to see where the conversation would go.

"No," Jenny insisted firmly. "She hadn't done that stuff in a long while."

Her husband's eyes welled with tears. "You knew?"

"Of course I did. She was my girl. A mother knows. But she swore to me she was getting help. I believe... believed her." She clenched and unclenched her hands. "I still do."

"Oh, Jenny." Reagan walked over to his wife and took her hand. "They found oxycodone and fentanyl in her blood, darlin'. That's not something you're going to find in someone who's getting help. What makes more sense, that someone killed her or that she fell into the lake somewhere because she wasn't in her right mind?"

So, Reagan McKay knew about the drugs, and he'd kept it from his wife. I knew he was trying to protect her, but buried secrets had a way of unearthing themselves. And what about the pregnancy? Was that something the police would have told them already? Reese hadn't known until today, and so far in this conversation, it hadn't come up.

"Fiona's drowning might have been an accident," I said. "But there was something else going on with her. Did you know she was planning to leave town?" I asked them.

"Where in the world would she go?" Jenny asked.

Reagan sucked his teeth. "Our girl didn't have two nickels to rub together. She spent money like it was burning her fingertips. It's why we had to cut her off."

"That's not all," Reese said. "She was—" I got the sense she was about to drop the pregnancy bomb, but Ezra cleared his throat and gave her a head tilt.

Reese gave him a sidelong look. "Can you give us a minute?" she asked her aunt and uncle. We all walked to the other side of the pool and out of earshot of Fiona's parents and their friends.

"I'm not sure it's a good idea to tell your aunt and uncle about Fiona's...situation." He glanced over at the group. "Reagan doesn't want to believe it's anything more than accidental."

"Fiona has put them both through a lot, Easy. But he

loved her. She was his world. Don't let his manner tell you different. It's just his way."

"I was here yesterday," Ezra said. "I know his mourning is real. But you've got Big Don and this Jameson fellow over there, and their wives. Laying our cards on the table is a dangerous move. There's a chance one of them is involved in all this mess. We shouldn't give all the goods away." He tapped the drive in his pocket and eyed Reese.

"We're talking about my cousin," she said, clenching her fists at her sides in frustration.

"You're either law enforcement in this situation or you're not. I'll accept either and proceed as necessary."

Reese took a deep breath and then nodded her head curtly. "I'm a cop."

"Then be a cop if you want to help your cousin," Ezra said.

"That's not fair," she seethed. "They're my family. But I agree. I don't like it, but I agree."

It was difficult to be on Ezra's side right now, because asking Reese to hold back information from her family was a hard pill to swallow, but we needed to keep some of what we knew on lockdown. "Reese, I understand how hard this is. Believe me. But you came to me for help. We still don't have any concrete evidence for you guys to open an official investigation. Too much knowledge in the wrong hands might lose you any evidence that might still exist." Like where Reese's ruby and diamond ring had gone. "When this is over, you can tell them everything."

She sighed then reached around her head and tightened her ponytail as if readying to get down to business. "We came here to look at Fiona's quarters. We should do that."

I nodded. "That's a good plan."

I'D BEEN HALF afraid that the McKays wouldn't let us into Fiona's space, not after Ezra had demanded that Reagan make us a list of every GCE member. I couldn't help but cringe at the idea of the Garden Cove Elite men's group being suspects. It smacked of a secret society built for the wealthy and powerful, so many of whom believed they were above the law.

I couldn't imagine Reagan protecting any of the members if he would have had knowledge that they'd been corrupting his daughter, though. But terrible things happened in this world, and sometimes that terrible was perpetrated by family.

I shivered. The idealistic view I'd once held of Garden Cove faded even more.

Hell, at this rate it would soon be ash.

Jenny had come to the guesthouse with us. "If you find anything, I want to be there," she'd explained, still pale and shaken. "I have a right."

Since this wasn't official police business, and no warrant was involved, it wasn't as if we could keep her away.

Reese's hand trembled so much she dropped the key.

Ezra picked it up. "I'll do it," he said. When he

reached for the handle, before he could even try to unlock it, it turned. "Huh. It's already open."

"I locked it up yesterday when I left. I know I did." Reese circled to her aunt. "Has anyone been in her since I left yesterday?"

"I've only let you in," Jenny said. "Maybe you forgot to lock it."

Ezra opened the door. "Oh, man," he said. "Was the place like this yesterday?" He went inside, with the rest of us right behind him.

The guesthouse had an open living room and kitchen space. Couch cushions littered the floor, end tables were overturned, and a picture of the lake had been torn off the wall.

"Who would do this?" Reese asked as she headed down the short hallway.

"And how?" I added.

This gated subdivision had a crap-ton of security. I couldn't see anyone just driving up and breaking in without some alarm or camera picking it up. It looked as if the place had been searched thoroughly, but not with the same viciousness that had been employed on my house.

Had it been Sideburns Guy? Or Boots Guy? Or maybe even the new player introduced in the last vision? I thought because Sideburns Guy been coming into the store for a couple of weeks, he couldn't possibly have anything to do with Fiona, but what if I was wrong? What if him stalking me and Fiona's death were linked somehow? The only common denominator we had was that both of us had been afraid of Phil Williams.

Jenny left the guesthouse looking as horrified as I felt. I was still reeling from the violation on *my* home. *Run, Jenny,* I thought. If I could've, I would've run, too.

Reese came back into the living room. "The bedroom and bathroom have been picked over as well." Softly, she asked, "Do you think this is about Fiona's flash drive you all found in Nora's purse?"

Ezra eyes darkened. He glanced around the space. "Probably."

Jenny came back with Reagan. Jameson and Big Don were on their tail. "I've called the police," Reagan said. "The real ones."

Ouch, that hurt. It wasn't as if our presence had caused someone to break in without being seen at all.

"Good." Ezra dropped into detective mode. "I was going to call them, so you've saved me a step. Officer McKay, could you move everyone out of here and secure the scene. Until we get gloves and foot covers, no one is allowed in or out of the place. Got it?"

"Yes, Detective Holden." She turned to her family and their friends. "Everyone out."

I guess Ezra and Reese decided to show Reagan just how real they were. "What about me?" I asked.

"You should wait outside, too, Nora."

"That's absolutely fine." I didn't want to be there, anyhow. It brought my awful morning rushing back to me, so Ezra didn't have to ask me twice to go.

I stood with Jenny and her gal pals, just a few feet away from the husbands.

"I can't believe this is happening," Jenny said. Her tone was sharp and choppy. "What is going on? It doesn't feel real." Tears flooded her eyes. "I keep expecting my baby to come home and complain about her job or tell me about some cute shirt she bought. And now she's gone. And this..." She gestured to the guesthouse.

I examined the area for surveillance. I still couldn't believe someone managed to get onto this estate and break in without notice. "Do you have video cameras or alarms?"

Jenny nodded. "Yes to both."

"Wouldn't they have been triggered?"

Reagan overheard my question and stepped over to join us. "There's only one way anyone could have gotten up here without us being alerted. They had to have come from the dock and taken the path through the woods."

"You don't have a camera set up back there?"

He scowled, his round face red with fury. "It's my own fault," he said. "Fiona was always unhooking and deactivating the back cameras and alarms. After I called the police, I checked my security monitors. The guesthouse and dock cameras are off. Fiona must have disconnected them the night she—" He choked on a ragged sob, spittle gathering on his lower lip as the sound of his grief became almost an animal-like wail.

"Oh, Reagan." Jenny threw her arms around her husband. He pressed his face against his wife's shoulders, his crying akin to a seal's bark.

"I'm so sorry," I said as I backed away, their sorrow

threatening to swallow me. "So, so sorry." God, I needed air. Lots and lots of it.

Everyone was so focused on the McKays, they didn't notice me walk off. I went around the guesthouse looking for the camera Reagan had been talking about. Sure enough, there was a video camera mounted on the siding. I saw the path to the dock and began the walk down.

When I got to the dock, I saw a boat moored to a rock on the shore a few yards away. I thought it strange that someone wouldn't have tied it to the dock. I went over and studied it. It was an aluminum Jon boat, about twelve feet long, with a small motor off the back. I smiled as I thought of my dad taking me out on the lake to fish in a similar boat. I wondered if Reagan had ever taken Fiona fishing.

I pressed a hand to my chest and closed my eyes as the gash inside me opened wide at his grief, and I fought hard not to cry. This wasn't my loss, I reminded myself. Yet, I felt it to my soul.

There was a small tarp in the boat. Carefully, I dipped down, trying to use my bad knees so I didn't further hurt my bad back, and I lifted it up.

My mouth went dry, my lips thinning with shock as I retrieved a red high heel. The kind someone might wear if they were dressed in a beautiful red cocktail dress.

I looked around quickly to make sure I was alone then pulled the tarp back more.

I saw a glint of gold in one of the crevices. I leaned in, ignoring the ache in my back, and dug into the spot, the golden item slipping from my fingers with every attempt. I used my fingernails to dig and was able to finally snag the object. I fished it up—both triumphant and horrified to discover the ruby and diamond ring.

The pungent musk of murky lake water made me dizzy.

A man gently lays a woman into the Jon boat.

"It'll be quick, Fiona," he says. "I told you he wouldn't let you get away with it. The drugs I put in your soda will make it real nice, though."

She moans, but he continues to untie the ropes and pushes the boat away from shore. She's not dead. Not yet. But she's barely moving. I watch her hands, folded together as she slowly works the ring off her finger and drops it into the boat without the man noticing. After he climbs inside, he covers her with a tarp, starts the small motor, and trolls away.

I'd watched for several seconds until they disappeared, helpless to stop it.

"He drugged her and killed her," I said. I squeezed the ring into my palm. "That poor, poor girl."

"You love snooping around, don't you?" The sinister voice came from a man who walked out of the tree line.

I snapped up, the motion wrenching my back. I stumbled and fell on my butt. I narrowed my gaze on the man, his gray sideburns prominent. Damn it, it was my not so friendly neighborhood stalker, Sideburns Guy. He wore gloves and was holding a gun.

Son-of-a-bitch. It was *my* gun.

CHAPTER 19

"Who are you, and why in the hell are you following me?" I asked, closing my fist around the ring. As I climbed to my feet, I managed to tuck the ring into my pants pocket.

The gun in Sideburns Guy's hand never wavered. I had no doubt he knew how to use it. My heart pumped in my chest so loudly, I was sure he could hear it. What would happen if I screamed? Would anyone hear me before I got shot?

"Where's the USB drive?" he asked in a deadly calm tone that made me shiver.

"I don't know what you're talking about."

"Yes, you do." He took two long strides forward. He kept the gun aimed at my center mass and used his free hand to make a gimme motion. "Toss me your purse."

I slid the purse off my shoulder and threw it at his feet. "Take it and go."

Sideburns chuckled. "This isn't a mugging, *Nora*. This is a fact-finding mission, and I'm not going anywhere. Neither are you. The USB drive wasn't at Fiona's house, or yours. That means you've been carrying it with you."

"I'm at a slight disadvantage seeing as how you know my name and I don't know yours," I said, hoping to buy some time.

"Let's leave it that way," he replied with a slight smile.

Fine. I'd just keep him talking and pray Ezra noticed I was missing. "If you destroyed my house looking for something I don't have, then you wasted a lot of energy on nothing."

"I saw the pharmacy security video, *Nora*." He picked up my purse and dumped it out, while keeping his gaze and the gun trained on me. All the contents clattered to the rocky beach, and once again, I felt violated by this man. He'd shattered my feeling of safety and security when he'd wrecked my home. And he was finishing the job by toeing through personal items, smashing my things with the heel of his shoe. "Fiona dropped the drive into your purse at Craymore's. Are you going to keep lying to me?"

Yes, I thought sourly. "You know there's a whole bunch of cops coming. If you shoot me, they'll be down here in less than minute. You'll never get away."

"I will, actually," he said. "Don't you know? I'm one of the good guys." He kicked my empty purse. "It's not here. Tell me what you did with the USB drive, Nora."

The way he kept saying my name, like we were pals, gave me the willies. "You're a cop."

He smiled. "It'll be a real shame when I find your body. Shot with your own gun."

I pressed my trembling lips together, trying to stave off the terror instilled by his threat. Gawd. I didn't recognize him as a cop for Garden Cove PD, but I didn't know everyone who worked there. Did Garden Cove have another officer on the take? Cripes, Shawn needed to give his department a thorough cleaning to get rid of all the dirty cops. "People will notice I'm gone soon."

Sideburns pulled a phone from his back pocket. While holding it with his non-gun hand, he expertly typed a message. His phone buzzed a few seconds later. He smiled at me. "No one's looking for you, Nora."

Who had he texted? It had to be someone at the house, right? It was the only way he could know I wasn't missed. And someone had noticed I was gone—maybe even called Sideburns to let him know I was on my own.

Did the McKays keep a staff on hand? Probably. The house was too big for Jenny to keep up on her own. Or maybe it was one of the friends. Was he working for the man who'd gotten Fiona pregnant?

"What is it with dirty cops?" I asked. "Why put on a badge at all?"

"Lots of reasons." He shook his head. "Fiona had a sweet deal after her arrest. All she had to do was mind her own business. But she couldn't do that."

"She was clean," I said. "No thanks to you." He wore cheap rubber waders on his feet. "Where are your tacky red and black boots now?"

He squinted at me. His confusion evident. "I don't know what you're talking about."

So not Boots Guy. Another thought occurred to me. He'd mentioned her arrest. According to Shawn, there had only been two people who knew about Fiona's arrest, but only one of them had seen her for monthly check-ins and a drug screens. Son-of-a—

This had to be the detective from Rasfield who had arrested Fiona. "Detective Frank Lopez," I bluffed. "Nice to meet you."

His eyes widened. Then he waved me off with his free hand. "You're never going to get the chance to tell anyone."

"How did you even know I'd be down here?" Was he somehow following me? Maybe tracking my phone? Ugh.

"It's not all about you, Nora. I was here to collect a payment left for me down here at the dock. You showing up is just a happy accident."

His phone buzzed again. He squinted down at it. "Time's up," he said. "Cops are here, and we have to go." He used the gun to point at the boat. "Get in."

Fear is a powerful motivator, but I wasn't some dumb innocent. I remembered my father's words of wisdom. *Baby, if you are being threatened, do what you have to do to survive the moment, but never, ever let a man take you somewhere else. No matter what he promises, no matter how much he threatens or cajoles. It's the surest way to certain death.*

I didn't need the reminder, though. I knew if I got into the boat with Sideburns, I'd end up like Fiona. I couldn't let that happen. If this asshole was going to take me out, he'd have to do it here and now and risk getting caught. But I was betting someone like him, someone motivated by money and little else, wouldn't take the chance.

My pulse drummed in my ears as I worked up the courage to make my stand. I planted my feet as solidly as I could on the rocky ground. "You're nuts if you think I'm getting in there with you," I said. "You want to drown me like you did that poor girl, well tough shit. Shoot me here and now. But don't forget, there are a handful of police officers just over that hill. I wonder how fast they can run down here? It only took me a minute or so to walk it. And I'm real slow."

I glanced up the hill. I could see the roof of the guesthouse, but not a person in sight. Where was my hot detective when I needed him?

"You're so brave, Nora," he said, completely unimpressed with my fake bravado. "Unfortunately, that and a buck fifty will get you a soda. I'll beat you to death with the butt of your own gun. No muss, no fuss." He took a step closer. "How many strikes will it take, do you think?"

He lunged at me.

I screamed my flippin' head off as I tried to sidestep him, tripped on a rock and went down like a fifty-one-year-old lead balloon. Lopez was not ready for middle-aged klutziness, and he tripped over my foot and rolled down the embankment. I spun to get on my hands and feet before he could get up.

"I'm glad I stocked up on shampoo, Nora, because

you won't be around to make any more." Lopez was already on his feet, aiming my 9mm at me. "This is the end for you."

"Help!" I bellowed while crawling away.

A gunshot exploded.

I dropped flat to the ground, my face splatting into a cake of mud. I waited for the pain to blossom the way it did the last time.

And I waited.

There was nothing. No pain at all.

"Nora!" Ezra rushed out of the woods on the left side of the path. He had his shirt untucked and a pistol in his hand. "Stay down," he ordered. "Stay down until I clear him."

I pushed myself over and looked down the hill where Sideburns had fixed me in his sights. He was on the ground, and his shirt was wet with blood.

Ezra kicked my gun away from Lopez, and he held his own weapon on the downed man. Reese came out of the woods from the other side, brandishing her sidearm as she jogged down to Ezra.

"Who is he?" Reese asked. "He looks familiar but..."

I sat up. "Frank Lopez. He's a detective from Rasfield."

Ezra cast me a meaningful look. "I'll let Rafferty know, so he can give the chief over there a courtesy call."

"You can't be serious?" Reese assessed the scene, put her pistol in its holster and took out her cuffs as she walked over to the downed man. "Another dirty cop?"

Ezra's worried gaze fell on me. "You won't need the

handcuffs," he said to Reese. "But we *will* need to call a coroner. He's dead."

Jeanna Treece had arrived with her partner, Levi Walters. "Are you okay, Ms. Black? Do you need to go to the hospital?"

I needed a hospital, but the kind for your head, not your body, because I was pretty sure I was having a nervous breakdown. "He killed Fiona," I said. "He slipped her the drugs and took her out in that boat. I found her shoe in there."

Ezra let Reese guard the dead dirty cop—it wasn't like he was going anywhere—and my hero knelt down next to me.

"Nora, my love." He picked leaves and twigs from my hair then used the untucked part of his shirt to wipe the dirt from my face. "You have to stop wandering off alone."

"It's not like I go looking for trouble," I said. "And trouble seems to be cops on the take. At least it wasn't Garden Cove this time."

"Don't worry about that now, sweetheart." Ezra caressed my cheek. "I want you to get checked over. I don't suppose you'd be willing to go to the ER?"

"I'm fine," I said. I didn't relish the idea of meeting with Dr. Allen's disapproving bedside manner anytime soon. "I actually don't feel all that bad."

"You're probably in shock."

"Could be," I agreed. I gestured down to where Lopez lie dead. "He was looking for the drive. He was working for whoever Fiona was blackmailing." I glanced around me and whispered, "He was texting with someone at the house. Check his phone."

"Be right back." He got up and asked Jeanna Treece for gloves. After he put them on, he picked up the cellphone, then came back to me. "He was texting a number. No name, though. And you're right. It looks like whoever it was, they were feeding him info." He gestured to Jeanna. "You and Levi head up to the house and confiscate every cellphone on the premises. If anyone tries to argue, arrest them. I'll take the heat."

"Yes, sir," Jeanna said, then she and her partner took off up the hill.

Ezra squinted at the phone. "This is not good."

"Let me see." I had to know if whoever the boss was, he'd ordered my death.

Ezra nodded. He held the phone up to my face.

All I saw was fuzzy, blurry, unreadable texts.

"Well?" Ezra asked.

"Well, I can't see jack-crap without my glasses," I muttered. Luckily, I'd put them in a sturdy glasses case and Lopez hadn't taken his boot to them. An inappropriate burble of laughter rose from that scared place inside me. "He was going to kill me, Ezra."

My guy nodded, and without any sugarcoating, he said, "Yes, he was."

"But you shot the shit out of him first."

The corner of Ezra's lip curled up in a half smile. "Yes, I did."

"I think I'd like to keep you," I told him. "You're extremely handy in a life or death situation and have other...uhm...attributes I'm fond of as well."

"Like my eggplant emoji?" he inquired.

I giggled at the reference. "Just like." The adrenaline waned and fatigue set in. "I'm going to need some clothes from my house. I'll stay with Gilly until my brain tells me it's safe to go home."

"You need to make a statement, but I'd like, when this is all said and done, for you to come home with me. I'll take you over to your place to grab any clothes and stuff you need. I'm not saying move in," he said quickly. "I know you like your independence. I just want you to know that you're safe with me."

"And Mason."

"Mason won't mind."

I worried the kid might. Still, I nodded.

"Is that a yes?"

"Temporarily," I answered. "Yes." Staying with Ezra for a few days would be an interesting test for our relationship.

He helped me to my feet and supported me as we walked up the path. "I'd really like people to stop pulling guns on me," I said.

"A lofty goal for a gal who courts danger on a regular basis," he said with a chuckle. He stopped and pulled me into his arms. "When you screamed, it was all I could do to hold it together. Instinct was the only thing that kept me from blundering in and getting us both killed."

"I was scared, too," I said. "But he's dead and we're alive." I kissed him. "We're both alive. Thanks to you."

When we reached the house, Reagan, Big Don, and Jameson hurried to us.

"Land sakes, Nora," Big Don said. "You look like you took a turn in a pig wrestling contest."

"Don't you know, I took first prize." Meaning, I was alive, so I won. I eyed all the men suspiciously, trying to figure out which one of them, if any, had sent the texts to Lopez.

Jenny joined us, and I softened my expression. "Detective Frank Lopez killed Fiona. He's dead now, but...he said he'd had to drug her soda. She wasn't drinking or getting high. It wasn't an accident. She was murdered." He hadn't exactly confessed, but I'd seen enough in my vision that I would testify that the words had come from the bastard's own mouth. "Reese was right. You both were."

Jenny hugged me. "Thank you," she said with a mother's fierceness. "Thank you for fighting for my girl."

Claire Portman put her arm around Jenny's shoulder. "Nora, I'd like you to be my guest tonight for the fireworks and dinner. My treat. Portman's on the Lake has the best view of the display. And since my grandson, Mason, is coming out, you an Ezra should definitely come too."

"I have plans," I said. "But thank you."

I looked over at Ezra. I'd forgotten that Mason had been planning to be at Portman's tonight. His expression told me, he had as well. If our thinking was aligned, then there was no way in hell we were going to let Mason out of our sight. Not when we didn't know who Lopez was working for. I hoped with everything in me that Big Don wasn't part of whatever nefarious stuff had been happening in Garden Cove. I didn't want Mason to have to deal with a criminal grandfather.

"I'm afraid I'm going to have to cancel Mason's visit tonight," Ezra said. "We're going to watch the fireworks at home as a family."

"That's too bad," Claire said. She shook her head. "I was really looking forward to seeing him tonight, what with Roger and Kati abroad. It would have been nice to have the company. Is there anything I can say to change your mind?"

Claire was the kind of person who exuded warmth, and I'll admit, I liked her. But I was with Ezra on this one. Until we knew who was threatening me and him, it was better to keep Mason safe at home.

"Sorry, but no," Ezra replied politely.

"It sounds great." Even though it really didn't. I'd had enough excitement for a lifetime in the past couple of days, and besides, one of these GCE assholes wanted me dead. I wasn't going to make myself any more available than I had to. "But not tonight. Another time. Okay?"

"The offer stands," Claire said. "Anytime, and please give my grandson a kiss for me."

CHAPTER 20

J'd handed the ring over to Jeanna Treece to put in an evidence bag. She'd gathered the shoe as well. Ezra's officers had confiscated every phone on the premises and checked the numbers against Lopez's phone. Unfortunately, there hadn't been a match.

Officer Walters had called the paramedics at Ezra's insistence. They'd given me the once over, and other than a few bruises and a muddy face, I was surprisingly okay. My back still hurt a little, but I think the tramadol I'd taken earlier had kept me from feeling the worst of it.

We were there for another three hours as they gathered evidence, collected fingerprints from the McKays and their friends, and did a thorough top to bottom investigation of Fiona's place. And finally, Reese was the one who'd found the dead burner phone at the bottom of the pool. Any one of them could have dropped the phone in there during the commotion. And since the cameras were off, there was no surveillance of the deed. The techs would have to see if it could be dried out enough to collect any evidence.

After all the I's had been dotted, and the T's crossed, Ezra took me home.

I couldn't look at anything too long in my house, because it pained me in a way that no physical injury could match. It enraged me that Frank Lopez, on someone else's behest, demolished my home then tried to take my life.

"I wish we knew who Lopez had been texting." It really bothered me that someone up at the McKay place was neck deep in my near-death experience by the lake. Not to mention the proximity to Mason's grandparents. The last thing Kati and Roger's marriage needed was dealing with the fallout of whatever the GCE had been up to. "It had to be someone in that group. Not Reagan, though. Not Fiona's dad."

"What makes you so sure it's not him? He seemed awful insistent his daughter's death was an accident."

"If you had seen the way he broke down earlier, you wouldn't ask me that question. That man is in serious emotional torment."

"I'd agree with you," said Ezra, "but I've been a cop long enough to know grief isn't always proof of innocence. I called the chief, and Fiona's case is officially reopened." He shook his head. "But with Lloyd Briscoll being an ex-bad cop, and Grigsby, and Rasfield PDs Frank Lopez on the take, I don't know who we can trust. Whoever's behind this must have deep pockets. Unfortunately, sometimes money talks."

"I trust Shawn," I said.

"Do you?" he asked.

"With Leila's poor health, I think he was in uber protection mode. Stress can lead to poor decisions, you know," I said in Shawn's defense.

Ezra was quiet for a long moment as he mulled over what I'd said. "You might be right. I'm not crazy about it, but it is probably what happened. Still, I'm not sure what to do with the drive. Right now, I can't put all my trust in Shawn with what I know about how he's handled it thus far. I'm leaning toward calling the FBI. That way, I don't have to worry about someone bungling the case on purpose. Besides, I'm not sure anyone at the station could make heads or tails of those numbers. The FBI have forensic accountants who could probably decipher those spreadsheets in no time."

I nodded. "I'll back whatever play you want to make here." I heaved a sigh as I looked around. "Right now, I need a hot shower and some clean clothes." This morning, my underwear, along with all my clothing, had been strewn about the floor. It made me sick that Lopez had touched them. "I don't think I can put any of my clothes on until I've washed them."

"Hey," he said, soothing as he put his forearms over my shoulder and dipped down to kiss me. "It's okay. You don't have to worry about your clothes. We've got you covered."

"Yes, we do," Gilly said.

When I saw my BFF standing at the top of my staircase, my knees turned to jelly—thank heavens Ezra was there to hold me up—and I started bawling. Full on crocodile-tears, gasping-sobs, and snot-for-days bawling.

"Oh no," Gilly said.

"What's happening?" Pippa was on the staircase now and matching Gilly's pace as they rushed down to me.

"We've got you," Gilly said as she wrapped her arms around me. "We're here, and we got you."

Pippa came at me from behind, and between the two of them, they made us a Nora sandwich. We all cried for a minute then I wiped my face on Gilly's shoulder. She ewwed. Pippa giggled. Then all three of us started laughing.

Ezra sat on the bottom step of the stairway. He'd put everything back into my purse that had fallen out. Now, he was holding a tissue he'd fished from it as he patiently waited for the best friend brigade cry-fest to finish. After we untangled our huddle, he handed it to me. I wiped my face and blew my nose.

"What are you guys doing here?" I asked.

"Easy called," Pippa told me. "He threw up the BFF Bat Signal, and we donned our bestie capes, jumped in the BFF mobile and headed over."

"I've washed two loads of essentials, panties, bras, some jeans, socks, and some shirts. The first load is folded. The second load is in the dryer, but I'll get it when I go back up," Gilly said.

"When did Ezra call you?" It had only been about three hours since Lopez had attacked me and died for his effort. "And how did you know—"

"I was your assistant for years, Nora. You're quirky, but not completely unpredictable," Pippa said.

"I love you, guys. Thank you so much."

Gilly grinned. "That's what we do."

"You better tell her your news," Pippa said to Gilly.

"Gio invited us out to the Portman's on the Lake fireworks buffet and dinner as his guests. The kids, well, Marco, really wants to do it. I said yes."

Pippa went up on her toes. "It's a free fancy dinner and the best seats in town for the big fireworks display. He'd given Gilly a table for at least eight people. She insisted, so that you and Easy and Mason could join us, too."

Gilly and Pippa looked excited.

"I understand if you don't want to go, but I wanted to give you the option," Gilly said. "I'm sure you probably just want to crawl in bed."

"I do," I admitted. "After a shower." They didn't know that the Portmans along with several of their pals were suspects in my near demise, because I hadn't called them, Ezra had, and I'm sure he hadn't told them everything.

"Are you going to be okay with that? Have you talked to Ari?" I wasn't sure whether the girl had talked to her mother or not, yet. I didn't want to spill the beans before the teenager had a chance to do the right thing on her own. "It might be a good idea to do that first."

"You don't have to worry," Gilly said. "I know that Gio was back in town three weeks ago. It pisses me off that he didn't see his kids when he came, and that he exacted a promise from Ari to keep a secret from me, but you know what? I'm so over Giovanni Rossi. The hate is gone. The indifference has set in. Feels fantastic."

I laughed. "Well, hallelujah and pass the cheese, ding-dong the wicked Gio is dead...in your heart, that is." I still didn't feel great about them going to Portman's tonight, but at least they weren't targets for whoever was after me. There was no reason to think they'd be unsafe. Still. "The Portmans or one of their friends is responsible for Fiona's death. One of them tried to have me killed today."

"What?" Pippa said. "Easy." She turned to Ezra. "You didn't say that when you called."

"It's an ongoing investigation," he said. "I told you what I could, and now, Nora's told you the rest."

"Are you still in danger?" Gilly asked.

"Honestly, I don't know." I wasn't sure what the point of coming for me now would be. I mean, my place was tossed, I was tossed, and I no longer had the flash drive. I think telling Lopez to kill me sent a pretty strong signal that I was no long necessary to the equation. Even so, my friends had nothing to do with any of it. "If you go," I said. "Just stick together. No one go off alone. Strength in numbers and all that."

* * *

SINCE MY GAL pals had washed my clothes, I showered and changed at my house. I couldn't take picking mud chunks from my hair anymore, and besides that, I needed to change my hormone patch. It had been four days, one day too long, since I'd put on the last one, and

I was sure it had accounted for the crying jags. Not that they weren't warranted.

After, I put on jeans, a red crinoline blouse, and white tennis shoes. For the first time in hours, I felt myself.

On the drive over to Ezra's, I asked, "Will Mason be mad he can't go to Portman's on the Lake? What did he say when you told him?"

"I texted and told him that we'd be home soon to talk to him. He loves his grandparents, and the fact that they might be suspects is something he doesn't need to know. Still, telling him he can't go to Portman's tonight should happen face-to-face, so he can understand that I'm trying to do the right thing by keeping him home."

"That's a good idea."

Ezra parked his truck, and when we got inside, the television was off, and the small cabin was quiet. "Mason?" he called. The boy didn't answer.

"Maybe he's out back."

Ezra rushed through to the kitchen, and I heard him cuss.

"What's wrong?"

He held up a note. "His grandparents hired a car for him. Mason went to Portman's."

"What do you want to do?"

"I'm going to get him. You can stay here if you want. It would probably be smarter and I'd completely understand. You've had two awful days. And Mason's most likely safe, I just don't want to risk it." Worry darkened his eyes. "Better safe than sorry."

There was no debate in my mind what I choice I would make. "I'm going with you."

"Bad idea," Ezra said.

"I'm full of those," I replied with a wink. "I'm going with you."

He took my hand. "Thanks, Nora."

"We're in this together."

It didn't take long to hop in the truck and get on the road to the resort. However, traffic was a mess. When we arrived at Portman's on the Lake, the parking lot was filled with crowds of people carrying coolers and blankets down to the hillside to wait for the fireworks.

"Damn it," Ezra said, looking for a spot. "There's no spots open."

"There's employee parking around the side there." I pointed to an access road. "Go that way," I said. "It has direct access to the kitchen, and it will get us inside quicker."

When Ezra pulled around, there were two spots near a service entrance. He parked in the one that had *Reserved for R. Portman* on a sign. "Good call," he said.

"There's the kitchen steps." I gestured to the stairs about thirty feet away.

We passed through the restaurant kitchen. Gio scowled at me. I guess being down a cook had him swamped. I felt bad for Chad, but I had no sympathy for Gio.

"Just passing through," I said hurriedly.

When we went through the Players dining room, Phil Williams was talking to the Players' hostess. Twyla was twirling her hair and laughing as if everything he said was funny or charming.

It made me want to puke. I followed Ezra out the entrance to the elevators. *We're fine, we're fine*, I told myself. "We're all fine."

The elevator dinged and we rode it up to the sixth floor where the conference rooms had been converted into one gigantic dining hall. We weaved through tables, both of us searching intently for Mason.

"Nora!" Gilly shouted from five tables over. She, Pippa, Jordy, Marco, and Ari sat at a table big enough for ten people, and it was close to the buffet line without being right up on it. Mason was sitting with them, smiling as he and Ari looked at a phone screen. Were they flirting?

Gilly stopped my musing in its tracks. "I thought you weren't coming. We were surprised when Mason showed up."

I raised my brow. "So were we."

Ezra's shoulders relaxed when he saw his son was okay.

"Dad? What are you doing here?" Mason asked.

Ezra took his son aside. "We need to talk."

"Okay," Mason said. "What's up?"

Ezra's phone rang. He grabbed it out of its case on his belt. "It's work."

Mason's expression turned from annoyed to worried. "Am I in trouble?"

"Just stay here." Ezra took the call. "Detective Holden. Wait a minute. I can't hear you." He looked at

Mason. "I'm going to step out for a minute. Do not go anywhere."

"Go ahead." I glanced nervously around. "We're okay."

"Hey, Aunt Nora," Marco greeted. "Can you believe Dad got us this table? It's so cool, right?"

"It is fancy," I said, mildly impressed. "Gio made all this happen, huh?"

"Well, I thought you weren't coming," Claire Portman said as she walked up to the table. She was wearing a tailored red and gold, hand-beaded gown that fit her curvy figure like a glove. The neck was a conservative scoop that wrangled her large chest in, but the back had a daring plunge.

"What a lovely surprise. Where's Ezra? I'd like to thank him for allowing Mason to come stay with us tonight."

"He didn't," I said. "He got home to a note saying that you'd sent a car for Mason."

"Oh, dear." Claire looked sincerely upset. "I forgot. I ordered the car last week to pick him up. I didn't even think to cancel it. Not with everything that's happened. I just assumed when Mason arrived that it was with his father's blessing." She paled. "Can I sit with you all for a moment?"

CHAPTER 21

$\mathcal{M}$ ason walked around me and gave Claire a kiss on the cheek. "Hey, Grandma."

She patted his face. "This one is such a blessing." She appeared genuinely fond of Mason. "Go get yourself something to eat before you blow away," she told him.

Mason looked to me for guidance. Ezra was out in the hall pacing back and forth in the small area, moving whenever anyone got too close to him.

"Your dad said to stay put."

"The food line is right there." He pointed at the wall. "You can see me the whole time."

"I'll take him," Pippa said. She tapped Marco and Ari. "Go get in line, you two."

Jordy got up. "I'll go, too." He smiled sympathetically. "Can't have too many eyes."

"I'm staying with Nora." Gilly crossed her arms over her chest. "Mason's not the only one who needs a babysitter."

I grinned at her. "Thanks."

"Where's Ezra?" Claire asked, glancing around.

"Out there." I pointed to the hallway.

Claire sighed and patted my hand kindly. "You poor thing. I can only imagine how tired you must be after all that business this afternoon. What you did for Jenny today, that was something else. I'm sorry about Mason, too. I didn't even think."

I nodded. "I'm ready to sleep for a week." I sat down, my gaze constantly switching between Ezra and Mason.

Claire took the seat next to me. "Jenny's been my best friend since before she was a McKay and I became a Portman," she said wistfully. "It's awful what happened to you today, but I can't say I'm sad that it ended in the death of the man who took her child from her." She shivered and tugged at her ear. "I can't even imagine what I would do if something happened to my Roger."

I liked Claire. I liked the way she'd been there for her friend. I didn't like how suspicious this whole case was making me about the Garden Cove rich, or should I say, the Garden Cove Elite.

Gah. The moniker left a bitter taste in my mouth. Elite, in this case, was just another word for spoiled assholes.

I wondered if Claire's son Roger had a GCE watch. Even if he did, the only thing that even slightly connected Roger to Fiona was the rumor that he'd been having an affair with a waitress. Just because folks said it, didn't mean it was real. And there were many waitresses at the resort. However, Fiona's pregnancy complicated things a lot...giving far too many people a motive to get rid of her—even if she was the daughter of a GCE member.

I decided to probe Claire. Gently. Smart or not, I was already in knees deep, I may as well take the swim. "I bet Roger and Kati are having a good time in the Bahamas. Although, it's hard to beat the weather we've been having."

Claire glanced at me. "Maybe," she smiled anxiously. "I haven't heard from them in a few days, but I'm sure the phone reception isn't great where they are."

"In the Bahamas?"

"Umm...yes," she said, turning her gaze on me. "They'll probably be home soon." She looked back at the food line, where Mason, Ari, and Marco were scooping piles of food onto their plates. "That Mason is a good boy. When he came into our lives ten years ago, he really brightened my world. I always wanted more children, but it wasn't in the stars. Children are so magical, don't you agree?"

"Sure," I said. *As long as they're someone else's*, I mentally added.

Claire nodded. "Why don't you tell me about Ezra?"

Claire had zigged on me, when I'd expected a zag. I would have thought Mason or Kati had told her about him. "He's kind, thoughtful," I said. "Honest." I leaned in "And if you wait a few minutes, you can ask him yourself when he gets back over here. He's an open book." At least, that had been my experience. It was one of the things I loved about him. I never had to guess with Ezra. Not about his past, and not about what he was thinking.

Why was his phone call taking so long? Were they able to pull something off the phone that was found in the pool? He ducked his head in and gave me a "Where the hell is Mason?" look. I pointed to the buffet and he saw his boy nestled between one of my besties and the twins. He nodded at me and went back to the hall.

Claire smiled fondly in Ezra's direction. "I admire a man who pulls himself up by the bootstraps and makes his own way. From what Kati and Mason tell me, Ezra has had a fair bit to overcome. Only thirty-two, and already a detective. He's impressive."

She'd mentioned his age casually, so I tried not to take it wrong. I went back to Mason's response to mine and Ezra's age difference and let it console me. If it worked for men to fall in love with younger women, the opposite shouldn't be a big deal. If only polite society would just fall in line with the same thinking.

Claire grinned as if assessing my thoughts. "I'm not judging. Big Don is younger than me by eight years. When we married, it was the scandal of the town. You're an attractive woman, Nora. And smart. And strong-willed." She put her hand over mine. She was about my mother's age, maybe early to mid-seventies. But if I hadn't known her, I would have put her in her mid-sixties, tops. Her brunette hair and glamor makeup were flawless. The only thing that really aged her were the spots on her hands. "You remind me a little of myself."

"I'll take that as a compliment, Claire."

Movement behind Claire made me look up. I swallowed the hard knot in my throat as Phil Williams leaned down and brushed his lips over Claire's cheek. Cripes. I'd been so focused between watching Ezra and Mason, I'd failed to notice a snake approaching.

"How are you tonight, beautiful?" He was talking to Claire, but he stared at me as he said it. "You look good enough to eat." He nipped her ear with his teeth.

That compliment never sat well with me. It always conjured up images of women being roasted over open-fire spits, while men yanked hunks of flesh from the bodies to devour. Gross.

Claire cupped his face. "Don't be cheeky," she admonished him with a smile. "What are you up to tonight?"

"Just out here to enjoy the fireworks." He raised a brow at me.

"Have you met Nora Black?" she asked.

Phil extended his hand. "Not formally," he said with a wry smile. "How do you do, Nora Black?"

I gulped as the cuff of his jacket slid up his arm to reveal a watch with the GCE symbol on the face.

I didn't take his hand. Instead, I nodded. "I do very well."

He chuckled. "I'm sure you do."

Claire looked back and forth between us. "Am I missing something? You two seem to have some history."

"Nothing worth mentioning," I said. "But Mr. Williams here wrongfully fired my best friend Gilly."

"I admit I might have been hasty," Phil agreed. "But she had been arrested for murder. Having a homicidal spa manager is bad for business."

I bit my lip to keep myself from spitting in his face. He'd been the reason Lloyd had been killed; he'd known it wasn't Gilly's doing. "She's better off away from the Rose Palace now, anyway. You did me a favor by letting her go. I've been trying to get her to go into business with me for months."

Phil smirked, completely unfazed by my ire. "You're welcome," he said. "Maybe I can come up with a way for you to return the favor." He dipped down and kissed Claire's cheek again. "You ladies have a nice evening. I'll see you around, Nora."

I gave him the brightest and most sincere smile I could muster. "Not if I see you first."

"Oh my," Claire said, as the biggest criminal I knew, someone she was on cheek-kissing terms with, walked away. "That was some sizzle between you two. I didn't know whether you were going to make out or kill each other."

"I would never make out with Phil Williams," I said flatly.

"He hurt your best friend." She gave me an approving nod. "It's understandable." She squeezed my hand. "You have a lot of guts, Nora."

Right now, I would have liked less guts since the current ones were in knots. I couldn't stop thinking of Phil Williams and that damn watch. I hadn't been privy to the list of GCE members that Reagan had provided the police, but that watch was confirmation Phil Williams was on the membership list. But Phil wasn't a resort owner, not like Big Don. From what Gilly had told me, the Rose Palace was owned by an investment group. Phil merely managed the resort.

Phil wore a suit tonight, not exactly cowboy boot attire, and he had on patent leather loafers. I watched as Phil met with Big Don over by the chocolate fountain. He twirled a piece of pineapple on a stick as they talked. Then Phil ate the chocolate-covered pineapple hunk and followed Big Don out a side door.

"Nora," Claire said. "You have a far-off expression on your face. What are you thinking about?"

"Where does that side door go?"

"The bathrooms and the open balcony. It's a beautiful spot to watch the fireworks show."

"Ah, bathroom," I said. "That's what I need." I wasn't going to be stupid and follow Big Don and Phil down some dangerous rabbit hole, but I did want to see where they were going. Minor recon only. And I'd take Gilly with me. Pippa and Jordy could watch the kids. That way I could tell Ezra when he got done with his call, and then he could do the investigating. "I'll be right back."

I'D MOTIONED at Ezra to get his attention, but he waved me off. This was one serious phone call. It scared me to leave the crowded room of diners, but I didn't believe any of the GCE would try anything as long as I stayed where people were congregating.

"Come on, Gilly," I said.

"Where are we going?"

"To the bathroom."

"Is your back acting up again? Do you need help with your pants?"

"Your worry is touching and super embarrassing, but no," I added quickly. "I am employing the buddy system. There's safety in numbers."

There were several people milling about, so I felt safe enough to proceed. Pippa and Jordy would watch Mason and the twins. The end of the corridor opened to a large, stretched balcony overlooking the lake. I could see why Claire said it was the best seat in the house. There was a velvet rope across the open doors, with a sign that said, "VIP Members Only."

I grabbed Gilly and flattened myself against the wall next to the women's restroom. "Hide," I said.

"Where?"

I moved her in front of me. "Let's just act like we're talking."

"Nora, we are talking. We don't need to act."

Big Don, Phil Williams, Jameson Campbell, and Burt Adler had gathered down by the balcony entrance and were having a chat. They weren't yelling, but if eyes could scream, I'd swear Big Don would've been screaming at them all. Big Don got loud once and said, "I won't go down for this."

I put on my glasses then held my phone up like I was still texting, aimed it down the hall, and tried to record their interaction. Instead, I snapped a picture. It made a shutter noise.

"Stop that," Gilly said.

"I'm trying to record them."

"To what end?"

"One or more of those jerks tried to have me killed, and they are also responsible for Fiona's death, and the death of her unborn child," I said.

"I get it, but we can't hear them, so all recording is going to do is draw attention our way."

"Fine." The four men finished their quiet conversation and started up the corridor in my direction. "Oh, crap, they're coming this way."

Gilly opened the women's bathroom door and shoved me in. "Wait. I'll tell you when the coast is clear."

The toilet flushed, making me jump. My chest tightened with anxiety. I let out a breath of relief as Lucy "Lips" Campbell exited a stall. In the harsh glare of fluorescent lights, she looked haggard. And were her lips bigger than they had been this afternoon? Cripes. Did she have a plastic surgeon on standby?

She crossed to the mirror and fixed her lipstick. She smiled lazily. "Hello, Nora."

"Hi, Lucy."

She was wearing a pale-blue satin tank top that flattered her blonde hair and tan complexion. I made a show of washing my hands. "That color really suits you."

"Thanks," she said. "I like your top, too."

"I got it at Nordstrom when I worked in the city." I couldn't help but notice she hadn't washed her hands. It made me scrub my own hands twice as hard.

She put her lipstick away and gave her coif a final fluff. The motion moved her hair away from her ears, and I banged my thigh on the corner of the counter.

Lucy Jameson had on a pair of ruby and diamond earrings, and they were a perfect match to Fiona's ring. My throat constricted.

When she passed me, I saw a white powdery substance at the corner of her nose, and her pupils were dilated. "Is it cold in here?" she asked.

Was Lucy Campbell high? "The temperature is warm enough for me."

This near, I saw some sores on her upper arms that she'd covered with makeup, making the scabs look like crusty warts. Her breath smelled like fruity rotten eggs, and I noticed that her teeth were just a little too perfect, most likely veneers. Why hadn't I noticed at the McKays? Probably because I'd been focused on other things.

"Can I help you somewhere, Lucy? Are you feeling okay?"

"I'm fine," she said. "I'm always fine. Just ask Jameson. He'll tell you." I had to turn my head to avoid a direct hit of halitosis.

"Christ, pull yourself together, Aunt Lucy," a girl says. "You need some serious help."

A woman in a cornflower-blue sundress and honey-blonde hair holds out her hand. "Give me the damn memory stick, Fiona. I can't believe you stole it from me. After all I've done for you."

"You mean like getting me my first taste of meth? Yeah, you've been stellar. My life is in shambles thanks to you."

"I didn't force you to do it."

"I looked up to you. You were the cool aunt. I thought..." She shook her head. "It doesn't matter now. I'm getting my

money and I'm getting as far away from you and everyone else in Garden Cove as soon as possible."

"He'll never pay you," Lucy seethed, her hands balled into fists. "You won't see a dime."

"You better make sure he does," said Fiona. "Or I'll ruin you both."

A man comes into the room. He's wearing red and black cowboy boots. "What are you two getting up to?"

I blinked as the memory went away. Holy horrifying reveals, Jameson Campbell was Boot Guy.

Lucy's wide eyes were staring me down. "You know. Don't you? Fiona was pregnant with my husband's baby." She beat her fist against her chest. "My husband. I loved that girl. She was like my very own niece. And she betrayed me."

"It takes two to tango," I said. "And you loved her so much you got her hooked on drugs."

"I didn't make her." Big, fat tears rolled down her cheeks. "I didn't mean...I just wanted to hurt him. Hurt them. Like they hurt me." She threw her arms around me in a desperate hug. I thought it was to keep from falling down—until I felt two sharp stings go into my back, then there was a crippling jolt of pain that brought me hard to my knees.

CHAPTER 22

*W*ahshabah..." My mouth tingled as my torso jerked spasmodically. What the ever-loving hell was happening? When the pain stopped, I gaped at Lucy as she held me tight. Cripes, the woman was strong. She showed me a hot-pink personal Taser.

"I'm sorry, Nora. I didn't want to do this." Her glazed eyes stared at me. "Any of it."

It certainly felt like she wanted to do it. I tried to go loose and fall away from her, but she hit me again with the Taser, and the increased voltage sent agonizing shocks through my entire body. My heart was in my throat, and my breath exploded from my lungs when the shocks finally subsided. "Stop, please," I panted, hoarse with pain. "No more."

She moved the contact points to my upper back. "It'll be over soon."

Did she think she was going to stun me to death? That's not how stun guns worked. Although, people weren't made to withstand multiple hits of electricity in a short period of time. So maybe it would kill me. And maybe, I'd just wish I was dead.

My gaze darted back and forth as I tried to find something, anything that could help me, but Lucy zapped me again.

A series of grunts stuttered from my throat, each shock more vicious than the last, until my nerves were too overwhelmed to function right. My peripheral vision started to dim. My eyelids fluttered. *Don't go under*, I told myself. *Stay awake. Stay awake.* I knew that stun gun effects didn't last long, and the only way I would escape my second maniac of the day was to not let myself pass out.

Cripes! I was tempted to suggest she knock my head in. It was quicker and would hurt less. "You...don't..." My breaths were coming too hard and fast. Damn it. I was hyperventilating. My tongue felt as if it were made of cotton, but I tried again. "Doh...nt."

The door opened behind us. A fresh surge of hope ran through me as Gilly poked her head in. "Nora, coast is—" Her eyes flew wide. "Nora!"

Lucy went full-on narcotic ninja. She shrieked, dropped me to the floor, then kicked the door, sending Gilly back out into the corridor, the door slamming shut. She turned the bolt lock.

"Hel...hell..." Jayzus! I couldn't get the freaking word "help" out.

Gilly was banging on the door now, hollering my name. Then she stopped suddenly. Or maybe I'd lost my hearing from the many tasings.

"Drowning you would be quicker," Lucy said on a maniacal laugh. Her tone turned vicious. "If these toilets can easily accommodate that high and mighty head of yours."

I tried to crawl toward the door—*Death by Swirly* would not be the headline of my obituary—but Lucy grabbed my leg and started hauling me toward the first stall.

I let out a strangled sound.

Seriously stoned Lucy never faltered. She was cool as a freaking cucumber as she yanked me around and shoved me through the door.

"Nooo," I managed to grate out. I tasted the tang of warm blood in my mouth, and realized I'd bitten my tongue. I tried to hook my feet on the door as she towed me into the stall. But then the cow zapped me again.

Icy terror slid through me as Lucy's determination matched mine in a battle of wills.

"We're coming, Nora. Hang on," I heard Gilly shout from behind the door.

The effects of the Taser were wearing off. Or maybe I was becoming immune from her constant inoculations.

Lucy was mumbling to herself now about how when this was all over, things could go back to the way they were. The woman was having a complete mental melt-down, and she was going to take me with her.

I heard several people yelling beyond the door as Lucy shoved me up against the commode.

My breathing had somehow righted itself, and I could talk again with effort. I had to find a way to get through to Lucy, to stop her before she pushed me—well, my head—into the toilet, literally to the point of no return. She was high and heartbroken. I needed to say something that would give her pause. I hated that I'd let her get the upper hand in the first place. I knew how to defend myself, but that required having control of my limbs.

Lucy got down on her knees beside me and grabbed my hair to push my face into the water. I said the first thing I could think of to make her stop. "It...it wasn't..." Oh, God, my lungs felt like they were on fire, but I forced the rest out. "Not Jame...son's baby."

I had no idea if it was true or not, but it worked. Lucy stopped trying to push my head into the blue water. "What?" The hope in her eyes frightened me. The woman was deranged. "Fiona wasn't pregnant with Jameson's baby?"

I shook my head. "Not...his."

"That's good. She still had to die," she said almost sadly. "And so do you. Then everything will be okay."

The restroom door banged open. "Let her go!" Gilly said, as she, Pippa, and Claire appeared at the open stall door.

"Lucy? What the hell are you doing?" asked Claire with the bathroom key in her hand. "Let her go. You're hurting her."

"That's the point," said Lucy, grabbing a handful of my hair as she pointed the Taser at the three ladies. "She's got to die. The last one," she slurred. "Promise."

Claire reared back, dumbfounded. "Lucy. Why are you doing this?"

"She's...crazy," I managed. Speaking of crazy, why had Gilly enlisted Claire and Pippa for help? Why not get Ezra? "Ez—"

Lucy put the Taser against my throat. "Shut up," she snapped.

It had been a minute since the last jolt, and I'd regained some strength back in my arms. I steeled my will and waited for my chance. It came when the door slammed open again, and Ezra charged inside, weapon drawn.

Lucy yipped and loosened her grip. It was the chance I needed.

I lurched forward, using my entire back to twist hard and land an elbow to Lucy's mouth. The minute she let me go, I slapped the Taser out of her hand. The tiny pink weapon slid under the wall into the next stall.

Gilly grabbed my feet that were sticking out of the stall and yanked me hard until I was out of the stall. Claire, who was surprising swift for a septuagenarian, slammed the stall door shut on her friend. Then Pippa braced herself against the door to keep it shut.

"Nora?" Ezra dropped to the floor beside me. "What happened?" He began examining me. "Jesus, you have burn marks."

"She's," I huffed. "Bad...person." I pointed to the closed stall where Lucy was captured, her mighty meth powers no match for my three determined saviors.

Two uniformed officers came in after Ezra. He pointed to Pippa. "Go relieve the civilian and arrest the woman in the bathroom stall for assault, kidnapping, and attempted murder. Those will do for a start."

I held Ezra's hand to my chest. "What t-took... so...long?"

"I tried to find you," Gilly said breathlessly. "You didn't answer my texts."

"I didn't get off the phone until a minute ago. I didn't get any of the dozen texts you sent until then." He smoothed my hair. "How does someone get taken captive in a commode? And how did you three get involved?"

"I was hiding," I said, my breathing finally returning to normal. "Gilly pushed me in here to avoid the GCE, and Lucy was...already..." I sucked in a breath. "Already in here."

"Well, how was I to know? I looked for you first," Gilly said to Ezra. "When I couldn't find you, I did the best I could."

"You did great." Ezra gripped my elbow. "You okay to stand?"

"Yes." I looked at him. "The kids?"

"Are with Gio and Jordy," Pippa said.

Ezra looked as relieved as me. "Thanks, Pippa." He helped me to my feet.

Pippa gave Gilly a hand up.

I reached back to my BFF and gave her hand a quick squeeze. "Thank...you."

I didn't cry. I was all cried out.

"What in the world? Someone explain what is going on out here?" Big Don Portman stood just outside the bathroom door, wearing an expression of outrage and horror.

One of the uniforms took Lucy out in cuffs to a chorus of relieved sounds from Gilly, Pippa, and Claire. The struggle had been too real.

I heard Jameson out in the hallway. "Get out of my way," he said. "Get your hands off my wife!"

I followed Ezra out of the restroom and glared at Jameson. "Your wife..." I poked my finger at him. "She tried to kill me."

"That's preposterous," Jameson blustered.

"Having an affair with a friend's daughter, that's preposterous," I accused. "You should...be ashamed." I leaned on Ezra, my knees a bit wobbly. "You and your wife ruined her. You ruined Fiona's life, and I hope you pay for it the rest of yours."

"They will," Ezra said. A murmur of voices grew louder as six uniformed police officers came running down the hall.

"What is this, Holden?" Big Don asked in a friendly tone. "You've caught your man, or woman, in this case. Let the guests enjoy the rest of the night. This doesn't have to escalate."

"Actually," Ezra said, "it does."

Reese McKay strolled over, her handcuffs out. "Jameson Campbell, I am arresting you on the charges of money laundering, racketeering, and drug trafficking. You have the right to remain silent..."

She finished mirandizing him as the other officers took Big Don Portman, Phil Williams, and Burt Adler into custody.

Ezra hugged me tight. "Am I gonna have to put you in full body armor every time you leave the house?"

"Yes," I said, thinking it was the most brilliant suggestion I'd ever heard. "I swear this wasn't my fault. I swear I didn't go off alone, and I just went into the bathroom."

"I believe you." He smoothed my hair back. "I'm sorry it took so long. I was coordinating the arrests via phone."

"How? Why?"

"Reagan McKay. He turned himself in at the station. He didn't even ask for immunity when he rolled over on this bunch. He said Lopez was the GCE's guy, and if he was involved in Fiona's death, then it had to be one of his cronies. Instead of trying to figure it out, he turned on all of them."

Claire had gone completely pale. "I need to go," she said. "I need to be with Big Don."

"Claire, I'm so sorry," I said. "You helped save me."

The older woman nodded then hurried down the hall after her husband.

I looked at my two best friends in the world. "If you hadn't come along with the key...if you guys hadn't gotten here in time." The words to express my gratitude escaped me.

Gilly looked at me. "We are your tribe—your sisters —and we will always have your back."

A FEW DAYS of rest later, I was feeling so much better.

I'd had to postpone my luncheon with Leila, but I signed up for the bone marrow donation drive. It wasn't until Friday, so I had a little time to get all my strength back. The only burns I'd gotten were in places where Lucy had made contact with my exposed skin. Dr. Allen did run tests for my heart and enzymes and things like that, and I had been in a normal level.

When I'd twisted around to elbow Lucy in the mouth, I'd broken the spasm in my back, and it had barely bothered me since.

It was still too early to know what was going to happen to Lucy and the GCE, but if I had my way, they'd all be rotting in jail for the rest of their useless existences. I had a fondness for Claire Portman and Jenny McKay. I hoped they weren't involved in the GCE's dirty business. The relief I felt at having Phil Williams off the streets was substantial.

On a brighter note, I'd called a realtor to list my house, and I already had a new home in mind. Mr. Garners' vacant house. The one right next to Gilly's place. Bonus, it was a ranch home without any stairs!

"You guys about ready?" Ezra looked drop-dead sexy in his jeans and navy-blue t-shirt. He tapped his watch. "It's getting near six-thirty, traffic is bad, and dinner is at seven."

I slid my arms around his waist and wiggled against him. "We could still stay home."

"Ready!" Mason said as he skidded out of the second bedroom.

"Or not," I said with a smile as I let Ezra go. We were all going over to Gilly's house for a barbeque rib dinner followed by the new Marvel Universe movie. I was pretty sure Mason's excitement was equal parts Ari and the food.

Unlike his dad, Mason's clothes wore him. He had on a sweatshirt that swallowed his torso and was entirely too long for his height, but there was an alien on his t-shirt that said, Take me to your Tacos.

I laughed. "I love your shirt. Good choice."

Mason half-grinned. "Thanks." He gave me a fist bump. "Tacos rule."

"Peas drool," I finished. Yuck. Peas.

Ezra watched the exchange, a soft smile on his lips. "Come on, now. We don't want to be late."

Mason's phone rang. "It's Mom," he said excitedly. He'd had only brief contact with her since she'd gone on her trip. He answered. "Hey. Yes. Okay. Yep, I'm happy." He frowned. "I am," he said again. "Okay, see you in a couple of days." He lips spread in a wide grin after he hung up.

Mason had been upset about Big Don's arrest. Mostly because of how it would affect his grandmother. Claire had shown remarkable resilience in the face of her husband's disgrace, though, and she'd reassured Mason she'd be all right. Even so, it was nice to see him smiling.

"What was that about?" Ezra asked, a smile lighting up his face. Mason's grin was infectious.

"Mom and Roger haven't been in the Bahamas," the kid said. "I wasn't supposed to say anything just in case it didn't happen..."

"In case what didn't happen?"

Mason's phone dinged with a text. "They've been in India."

"Why?" Ezra asked.

He pulled it up and showed us. It was a message from his mom with a picture attached. The picture was of Roger and Kati, and a tiny little girl with shiny dark hair and brown eyes.

Mason smiled. "Mom and Roger have been trying to adopt for a while. They've had two that didn't happen. But this time, they're coming home with my new sister."

Ezra smiled. "I'm happy for them."

"This really is a cause for celebration," I said. "Let's get this party started."

Mason was out the door before us. I stopped Ezra. He put his arms around me. His bright green eyes, as he stared down at me, lit up my heart.

"What's on your mind?"

He tucked a lock of hair behind my ears. "It's strange thinking about Mason with a sibling that isn't, you know, mine."

I gazed up at him and smirked. "You know that uterine ship has sailed with me, right? And even if it hadn't—"

He laughed. "Good God, Nora. I don't want any more kids."

I chuckled. "Oh, thank heavens. Because for a moment, you had me worried."

"The only thing I'd enjoy about having a baby right now is the making part." His hand slid into my back pocket and he gave my derriere a firm squeeze.

I arched my brow. "Don't start nothing you can't finish, mister."

"There's a reason people call me Easy," he countered.

"Oh, I know just how easy you are." I went up on my toes and nipped his lower lip.

"Yes, you do." He wrapped me tighter into his arms, his hand cupping my neck. "I'm happier than I've been in a very long time."

"Me too," I said, my palms sliding down his backside. "Incredibly happy."

His voice grew husky with emotion. "I love you, Nora."

"Good." I sank into his embrace and let him kiss me until I was dizzy. "I love you too."

His truck horn blared, and we jumped apart like two school kids caught in the janitor's closet.

We looked at each other for a stunned second, then we both laugh. We'd gotten so caught up in the moment, we'd forgotten about Mason waiting for us in the car.

"Your boy's hungry," I said.

"He's always hungry." Ezra took my hand. "You ready?"

"For you?" I asked. "Absolutely."

The End

WAR OF THE NOSES

A NORA BLACK MIDLIFE PSYCHIC
MYSTERY BOOK 3

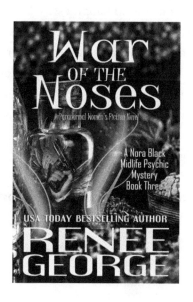

My name is Nora Black. I'm turning fifty-two,
but I don't feel a day over thirty-nine. That is,
when my feet don't hurt, my eyesight isn't failing,
and my scent-induced psychic ability isn't
showing me crimes.

For my birthday, my best friend Gilly signed us up for a weekend at the Central Midwest Spa Convention. Yay. Massages, fine dining, maid service, and best of all, as long as we attend a few workshops, the weekend is a tax write-off. It should be all sunshine and roses, right? Wrong.

It turns out that the Queen Maleficent of Makeup and my former nemesis , Carmen Carraway, is a featured presenter, and she seems determined to ruin my birthday weekend. But when a certain hot detective shows up to surprise me, I push aside my ill will and try to focus on my newfound happiness.

Unfortunately, a disturbing smell-o-vision of a gun and a threat has me trying to save Carmen rather than throttle her. When Gilly finds the murdered body of Carmen's assistant in a meditation pod, it's all noses on deck for this mystery. And I'll need all my senses to find out who wants to kill Carmen before she ends up dead. That is, if I don't kill her first.

www.norablackmysteries.com
August 2020

PIT PERFECT MURDER

BARKSIDE OF THE MOON COZY
MYSTERIES BOOK 1

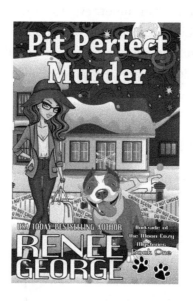

When cougar-shifter Lily Mason moves to Moonrise,
Missouri, she wishes for only three things from the
town and its human population. . . to find a job, to find
a place to live, and to live as a human, not a theri-
anthrope.

Lily gets more than she bargains for when a rescue pit bull named Smooshie rescues her from an oncoming car, and it's love at first sight. Thanks to Smooshie, Lily's first two wishes are granted by Parker Knowles, the owner of the Pit Bull Rescue center, who offers her a job at the shelter and the room over his garage for rent.

Lily's new life as an integrator is threatened when Smooshie finds Katherine Kapersky, the local church choir leader and head of the town council, dead in the field behind the rescue center. Unfortunately, there are more suspects than mourners for the elderly town leader. Can Lily keep her less-than-human status under wraps? Or will the killer, who has pulled off a nearly Pit Perfect murder, expose her to keep Lily and her dog from digging up the truth?

Chapter One

When I was eighteen years old, I came home from a sleepover and found my mom and dad with their throats cut, and their hearts ripped from their chests.

My little brother Danny was in a broom closet in the kitchen, his arms wrapped around his knees, and his face pale and ghostly. Until that day, I'd planned to go to college and study medicine after graduation, but instead, I ended up staying home and taking care of my seven-year-old brother.

Seventeen years later, my brother was murdered. At the time, Danny's death looked like it would go unsolved, much like my parents' had.

Without Haze Kinsey, my best friend since we were five, the killers would have gotten away with it. She was a special agent for the FBI for almost a decade, and when I called her about Danny's death, she dropped everything to come help me get him justice. The evil group of witches and Shifters responsible for the decimation of my family paid with their lives.

Yes. I said witches and Shifters. Did I forget to mention I'm a werecougar? Oh, and my friend Hazel is a witch. Recently, I discovered witches in my own family tree on my mother's side. Shifters, in general, only mated with Shifters, but witches were the exception. As a matter of fact, my friend Haze is mated to a bear Shifter.

I wouldn't have known about the witch in my genealogy, though, if a rogue witch coven hadn't done some funky hoodoo witchery to me. Apparently, the spell activated a latent talent that had been dormant in my hybrid genes.

My ancestor's magic acted like truth serum to anyone who came near her. No one could lie in her presence. Lucky me, my ability was a much lesser form of hers. People didn't have to tell me the truth, but whenever they were around me, they had the compulsion to overshare all sorts of private matters about themselves. This can get seriously uncomfortable for all parties involved. Like, the fact that I didn't need to know that Janet Strickland had been wearing the same pair of underwear for an entire week, or that Mike Dandridge had sexual fantasies about clowns.

My newfound talent made me unpopular and unwelcome in a town full of paranormal creatures who thrived on little deceptions. So, when Haze discovered the whereabouts of my dad's brother, a guy I hadn't known even existed, I sold all my belongings, let the bank have my parents' house, jumped in my truck, and headed south.

After two days and 700 miles of nonstop gray, snowy weather, I pulled my screeching green and yellow mini-truck into an auto repair shop called The Rusty Wrench. Much like my beloved pickup, I'd needed a new start, and moving to a small town occupied by humans seemed the best shot. I'd barely made it to Moonrise, Missouri before my truck began its death throes. The vehicle protested the last 127 miles by sputtering to a halt as I rolled her into the closest spot.

The shop was a small white-brick building with a one-car garage off to the right side. A black SUV and a white compact car occupied two of the six parking spots.

A sign on the office door said: *No Credit Cards. Cash Only. Some Local Checks Accepted (Except from Earl—You Know Why, Earl! You check-bouncing bastard).*

A man in stained coveralls, wiping a greasy tool with a rag, came out the side door of the garage. He had a full head of wavy gray hair, bushy eyebrows over light blue, almost colorless eyes, and a minimally lined face that made me wonder about his age. I got out of the truck to greet him.

"Can I help you, miss?" His voice was soft and raspy with a strong accent that was not quite Deep South.

"Yes, please." I adjusted my puffy winter coat. "The

heater stopped working first. Then the truck started jerking for the last fifty miles or so."

He scratched his stubbly chin. "You could have thrown a rod, sheared the distributor, or you have a bad ignition module. That's pretty common on these trucks."

I blinked at him. I could name every muscle in the human body and twelve different kinds of viruses, but I didn't know a spark plug from a radiator cap. "And that all means..."

"If you threw a rod, the engine is toast. You'll need a new vehicle."

"Crap." I grimaced. "What if it's the other thingies?"

The scruffy mechanic shrugged. "A sheared distributor is an easy fix, but I have to order in the part, which means it won't get fixed for a couple of days. Best-case scenario, it's the ignition module. I have a few on hand. Could get you going in a couple of hours, but..." he looked over my shoulder at the truck and shook his head, "...I wouldn't get your hopes up."

I must've looked really forlorn because the guy said, "It might not need any parts. Let me take a look at it first. You can grab a cup of coffee across the street at Langdon's One-Stop."

He pointed to the gas station across the road. It didn't look like much. The pale-blue paint on the front of the building looked in need of a new coat, and the weather-beaten sign with the store's name on it had seen better days. There was a car at the gas pumps and a couple more in the parking lot, but not enough to call it busy.

I'd had enough of one-stops, though, thank you. The bathrooms had been horrible enough to make a wereraccoon yark, and it took a lot to make those garbage eaters sick. Besides, I wasn't just passing through Moonrise, Missouri.

"Have you ever heard of The Cat's Meow Café?" Saying the name out loud made me smile the way it had when Hazel had first said it to me. I'd followed my GPS into town, so I knew I wasn't too far away from the place.

"Just up the street about two blocks, take a right on Sterling Street. You can't miss it. I should have some news in about an hour or so, but take your time."

"Thank you, Mister..."

"Greer." He shoved the tool in his pocket. "Greer Knowles."

"I'm Lily Mason."

"Nice to meet ya," said Greer. "The place gets hoppin' around noon. That's when church lets out."

I looked at my phone. It was a little before noon now. "Good. I could go for something to eat. How are the burgers?"

"Best in town," he quipped.

I laughed. "Good enough."

Even in the sub-freezing temperature, my hands were sweating in my mittens. I wasn't sure what had me more nervous, leaving the town I grew up in for the first time in my life or meeting an uncle I'd never known existed.

I crossed a four-way intersection. One of the signs was missing, and I saw the four-by-four post had snapped off at its base. I hadn't noticed it on my way in. Crap. Had I run a stop sign? I walked the two blocks to Sterling. The diner was just where Greer had said. A blue truck, a green mini-coup, and a sheriff's SUV were parked out front.

An alarm dinged as the glass door opened to The Cat's Meow. Inside, there was a row of six booths along the wall, four tables that seated four out in the open floor, and counter seating with about eight cushioned black stools. The interior décor was rustic country with orange tabby kitsch everywhere. A man in blue jeans and a button-down shirt with a string tie sat in the nearest booth. A female police officer sat at a counter chair sipping coffee and eating a cinnamon roll. Two elderly women, one with snowball-white hair, the other a dyed strawberry-blonde, sat in a back booth.

The white poof-headed lady said, "This egg is not over-medium."

"Well, call the mayor," said Redhead. "You're unhappy with your eggs. Again."

"See this?" She pointed at the offending egg. "Slime, right here. Egg snot. You want to eat it?"

"If it'll make you shut up about breakfast food, I'll eat it and lick the plate."

A man with copper-colored hair and a thick beard, tall and well-muscled, stepped out of the kitchen. He wore a white apron around his waist, and he had on a black T-shirt and blue jeans. He held a plate with a single fried egg shining in the middle.

The old woman with the snowy hair blushed, her thin skin pinking up as he crossed the room to their table. "Here you go, Opal. Sorry 'bout the mix-up on your egg." He slid the plate in front of her. "This one is pure perfection." He grinned, his broad smile shining. "Just like you." He winked.

Opal giggled.

The redhead rolled her eyes. "You're as easy as the eggs."

"Oh, Pearl. You're just mad he didn't flirt with you."

As the women bickered over the definition of flirting, the cook glanced at me. He seemed startled to see me there. "You can sit anywhere," he said. "Just pick an open spot."

"I'm actually looking for someone," I told him.

"Who?"

"Daniel Mason." Saying his name gave me a hollow ache. My parents had named my brother Daniel, which told me my dad had loved his brother, even if he didn't speak about him.

The man's brows rose. "And why are you looking for him?"

I immediately knew he was a werecougar like me. The scent was the first clue, and his eyes glowing, just for a second, was another. "You're Daniel Mason, aren't you?"

He moved in closer to me and whispered barely audibly, but with my Shifter senses, I heard him loud and clear. "I go by Buzz these days."

"Who's your new friend, Buzz?" the policewoman asked. Now that she was looking up from her newspaper, I could see she was young.

He flashed a charming smile her way. "Never you

mind, Nadine." He gestured to a waitress, a middle-aged woman with sandy-colored hair, wearing a black T-shirt and a blue jean skirt. "Top off her coffee, Freda. Get Nadine's mind on something other than me."

"That'll be a tough 'un, Buzz." Freda laughed. "I don't think Deputy Booth comes here for the cooking."

"More like the cook," the elderly lady with the light strawberry-blonde hair said. She and her friend cackled.

The policewoman's cheeks turned a shade of crimson that flattered her chestnut-brown hair and pale complexion. "Y'all mind your P's and Q's."

Buzz chuckled and shook his head. He turned his attention back to me. "Why is a pretty young thing like you interested in plain ol' me?"

I detected a slight apprehension in his voice.

"If you're Buzz Mason, I'm Lily Mason, and you're my uncle."

The man narrowed his dark-emerald gaze at me. "I think we'd better talk in private."

Want more? Got to www. barksideofthemoonmysteries.com

PARANORMAL MYSTERIES &
ROMANCES

BY RENEE GEORGE

Nora Black Midlife Psychic Mysteries

www.norablackmysteries.com
Sense & Scent Ability (Book 1)
For Whom the Smell Tolls (Book 2)
War of the Noses (Book 3)

Peculiar Mysteries

www.peculiarmysteries.com
You've Got Tail (Book 1) FREE Download
My Furry Valentine (Book 2)
Thank You For Not Shifting (Book 3)
My Hairy Halloween (Book 4)
In the Midnight Howl (Book 5)
My Peculiar Road Trip (Magic & Mayhem) (Book 6)
Furred Lines (Book7)
My Wolfy Wedding (Book 8)
Who Let The Wolves Out? (Book 9)
My Thanksgiving Faux Paw (Book 10)

Witchin' Impossible Cozy Mysteries

www.witchinimpossible.com
Witchin' Impossible (Book 1)
Rogue Coven (Book 2)
Familiar Protocol (Booke 3)
Mr & Mrs. Shift (Book 4)

Barkside of the Moon Mysteries

www.barksideofthemoonmysteries.com
Pit Perfect Murder (Book 1)
Murder & The Money Pit (Book 2)
The Pit List Murders (Book 3)
Pit & Miss Murder (Book 4)
The Prune Pit Murder (Book 5)

Madder Than Hell

www.madder-than-hell.com
Gone With The Minion (Book 1)
Devil On A Hot Tin Roof (Book 2)
A Street Car Named Demonic (Book 3)

Hex Drive

https://www.renee-george.com/hex-drive-series
Hex Me, Baby, One More Time (Book 1)
Oops, I Hexed It Again (Book 2)
I Want Your Hex (Book 3)

Midnight Shifters

www.midnightshifters.com
Midnight Shift (Book 1)

The Bear Witch Project (Book 2)
A Door to Midnight (Book 3)
A Shade of Midnight (Book 4)
Midnight Before Christmas (Book 5)

ABOUT THE AUTHOR

I am a USA Today Bestselling author who writes paranormal mysteries and romances because I love all things whodunit, Otherworldly, and weird. Also, I wish my pittie, the adorable Kona Princess Warrior, and my beagle, Josie the Incontinent Princess, could talk. Or at least be more like Scooby-Doo and help me unmask villains at the haunted house up the street.

When I'm not writing about mystery-solving were-cougars or the adventures of a hapless psychic living among shapeshifters, I am preyed upon by stray kittens who end up living in my house because I can't say no to those sweet, furry faces. (Someone stop telling them where I live!)

I live in Mid-Missouri with my family and I spend my non-writing time doing really cool stuff...like watching TV and cleaning up dog poop

Follow Renee!
Bookbub
Renee's Rebel Readers FB Group
Newsletter